OTHER BOOKS BY CAT SPYDELL

Epona's Gift (Spring 2012)

Jenna's Rave (Summer 2012)

The Planted Seed (Fall 2012)

OTHER BOOKS BY
MISCHEVOUS MUSE PRESS
that you may enjoy

The Einstein Solution
by Jean Adair Shriver

The Lightbridge Legacy
by Elayne James

VISIT JESSIE ALLEN ON FACEBOOK!

www.facebook.com
The-Time-Travelers-Apprentice-at-Hollywood-High

THE
TIME TRAVELER'S
APPRENTICE

at Hollywood High

CAT SPYDELL

MISCHIEVOUS MUSE PRESS   WORLD NOUVEAU COMPANY

The Time Traveler's Apprentice
at Hollywood High
A Mischievous Muse Book / Nov. 2011

Published by Mischievous Muse Press
A Division of World Nouveau, Inc.
Los Angeles County, California

Library of Congress Cataloging-in-Publication Data
Spydell, Cat.
The Time Traveler's Apprentice / Cat Spydell
fantasy / young adult fiction

Cover design and photography
by Gineve Rudolph
Bio photo by J. Kevin Leach

Mischievous Muse Press/ World Nouveau Company
ISBN: 978-0-9828865-7-1

Printed in the United States of America

10 9 8 7 6 5 4 3 2 1

Acknowledgements

This one is for my children, Kodiak and Cassidy, who have always believed in me, and for my ever-patient mother, Billie, who is always there to pitch in to help me with my 'real life' when I am in the throes of a writing deadline. Special thanks to my weekly writing group, who have been there through every paragraph with their enlightening critiques. Also, a shout out to Stacey for showing me how, Sally for her hard work, and to Gineve, because without her, none of it would happen.

I dedicate this book to the late Helen Green, who told me to.

The
Time Traveler's
Apprentice
at Hollywood High

Chapter One

I flop onto my messy bed, hitting bare mattress instead of the crumpled sheet. I get back up and straighten the covers, tucking in the blankets, annoyed. Today's tortures crowd my brain and for the millionth time I wish I didn't have to go to high school. The only good thing about Hollywood High is my boyfriend Jimmy, but he's graduating next June. I really need to look into passing some GED test so I can escape too, I think as I slide back into my now-made bed and yank my comforter to my chin and breathe in a sigh, trying to forget about yet another lame-ass day. The usual pulsing glow of the Hollywood skyline beyond my window calms me like a lullaby when I snap off the bedside lamp.

Headlights illuminate my room. It's Mother, pulling into the driveway, home from her weekly meeting. My jaw clenches; I know she'll stop by my room to say goodnight. Maybe I will close my eyes and pretend to be asleep. I really don't have anything to say to her. Did she see the light go off? I hear her coming in, kicking off her heels, putting down her purse, the jangle of her keys up the stairs.

"Goodnight, Jessica," Mother calls from behind the closed door. She doesn't come in my room but I can feel her hovering in the doorway. "I know you're awake."

"'Night," I say in a tired voice, keeping my eyes shut as she opens the door.

"How was your day?"

"Fine."

"Homework done?"

"Yes."

"Get some sleep, then."

"I will."

There is a pause, as if she wants to say a quadrillion more things to me, and I know she does; that meeting was about me, after all. But neither of us is up for that kind of conversation. She closes the door and as I hear her walk down the hallway, my eyes pop open. Outside my window the palm trees bend, illuminated by street lamps and blown by soft Santa Ana winds. I watch the breeze moving leaves around, and hear the tinkling of wind chimes on our front porch. I breathe in to make myself relax, alone at last.

As I wait for sleep to take me, I hear a weird humming noise in my room. At first I assume it's the wind, but it's not a sound I've ever heard before. *Now what?* I sit up and look around, hoping to discover what that sound is, when my heart clutches in fear. I see a vague blue outline of . . . something . . . and realize there's a tall willowy figure standing at the foot of my bed, with big eyes staring at me! My first reaction is to scream but it sticks in my throat and I can't. My mouth is locked open like Edvard Munch's painting and I'm freaking out on the inside, but all of a sudden I get strangely calm, because somehow I now know

2

I don't need to scream because it is only my granddaughter. *Wait, what? My granddaughter? I can't have a granddaughter. I'm sixteen!* I'm completely flipped out because in my mind I am being told that this granddaughter of mine is, like, from millions of years in the future. My great-great-great-great-infinity.

"What are you doing here?" I ask in a shaky voice, recognizing her for who she is as if we'd just had a sit-down chat at Starbucks earlier and she'd forgotten to tell me something. I feel like I'm in a dream, but I know I'm awake.

"I am here to warn you, Jessica," she says in a voice that comes into my head without her opening her mouth. Not that she has a mouth, not really, just a small slit that could be either nose or mouth in the middle of her intelligent blue-gray face. Her luminous eyes bulge in the darkness. Now that I have my voice back I feel as if I should keep with my original plan and try screaming again, but suddenly I feel even calmer, as if she put some kind of mindspell on me. In a weird way she is beautiful and I am transfixed by her being.

"Warn me about what?" I ask, the shakiness in my voice gone, and when she blinks at me there is a small death as she closes her eyes, as if the lights have gone out. I realize I don't want her presence to leave me.

"You know who I am to you, because I have told you through telepathy," she says with her mind. "I am your kin of what you call the future; you are my direct ancestor. You are the link that brings myself and thousands of others forth into life. I have been searching for you. I am what you will become."

"You look like an alien," I tell her, wondering if that's an offensive thing to say. I used to watch *Roswell* as a kid before it was cancelled . . . I've seen pictures of aliens and she does

3

look like one . . . big head, big eyes, thin body. But the small flap in her nose/mouth region moves gently at the sides and I am amazed . . . she is smiling. My heart leaps with happiness at the sight of it. I must be under a spell, I'm not even afraid anymore as her words fill my head.

"We are, what many of you Early Humanoids, call aliens, but we are not from another galaxy . . . we are the Humans of, in your version of time and space, the future." Her words in my mind are slow and deliberate, as if she is trying to explain something very complex to someone very stupid. But I get it.

"Oh . . . cool! You mean, you can, like . . . time travel?" I've seen *Back to the Future* with my dad about a million times. That's "our" movie, so I'm no dummy about stuff like that.

"There is no such thing as Time . . ." she begins to explain, but she stops herself. Re-boot. I'm curious about what she means by that but she's too quick for me. "That is of no consequence now. I am here to warn you of your current relationship. You must use caution Jessica. You have many paths, and only one of them leads to me. The others . . ." Again with the already annoying habit of censoring herself. "The other paths lead to things I cannot tell you now. Heed my words: You must end your relationship with Jimmy Becker immediately. Our lives depend upon it."

I don't know what to think when she then touches me on my upper arm with three of her four long fingers, and her touch feels both chilly and hot at the same time. With a really cool wavery blue shimmer she vanishes and I'm all alone in my dark room wondering what the hell just happened. My eyes are bugging, almost as big as hers, as I think of what she said. Beware of my relationship with Jimmy Becker? What's my boyfriend got to do with my

4

future relatives? How can Jimmy be bad for me? Maybe I'm hallucinating-they did drug me up pretty good last year in the hospital. Maybe it's a flashback of some kind. My mind tumbleweeds as I finally fall into a fitful sleep.

"Jessica Allen, we're late! Get out of bed!" Mother screams into my bedroom as she runs through the hallway. I bolt upright, my heart racing. What the . . . ? I look at the clock. 7:40! Hell, my alarm didn't go off . . . again. I get up and throw off my nightshirt. I open the closet door--nothing to wear. Just last year's rags. Not even a decent shirt. I grab for the laundry pile under my bedroom window and start digging. I find my favorite jeans . . . just a hint of ketchup. Fixable. A retro "Foxy Lady" glitter T-shirt --totally wrinkled--I sniff the armpits . . . and stinky. Dryer sheet in the dryer? Maybe. Man, I'm so late! Yesterday's bra drapes the chair. I throw it on with some miraculously clean panties from my drawer and run downstairs toward the dryer with my laundry/outfit, barely remembering to grab my plugged-in cell in case I get a text from Kara or Jimmy. Thank God my undies are clean. I sponge off the ketchup stain on the knee of my jeans, put the T-shirt in the dryer with a fresh-scent sheet and get lucky finding my sandals by the refrigerator . . . no socks required, because finding a pair of matching socks in my house has eluded me since kindergarten and now I'm a sophomore in high school, so it's been a long time since I've worn matched socks. I'm dressed and scarfing down my Pop-Tart and OJ when my wretched brother Keith comes in and starts his morning harassment routine.

"So, Jimmy called, after you passed out last night. I told him I thought you took a drug overdose and might be dead."

"Did he really call?" I ask mildly, knowing Jimmy never calls our house phone; he just leaves me a message on my cell. My blood is starting to simmer anyway and I stare moodily at the kitchen knives for effect. Lucky for me I have gone off the deep end a couple times so Keither is really deep down afraid of me since I attempted suicide last year. My therapist, Michael, says he just hides his fear of me because my presence emasculates him, whatever that means. I think it has something to do with sex. I really don't want to know so I haven't asked Michael to explain. Thinking about Keith in that way just makes me ill. Keith sees me staring at the knives and he flinches. Round one, and I won it. That was almost too easy. But Keith isn't done with me yet.

"Mom!" Keith yells when Mother pops her head around the corner. Her eyes glaze and I recognize her Lost-Keys-in-the-Morning-Look. I suddenly remember a dream I had, a weird-ass dream about some ghost or something in my room. . . what the hell was that? I frown, trying to get the mental picture clear, but it's all a blur.

"What?" Mother is testy. I wouldn't be messing with her if I were Keith, but he likes to "ride on the edge," as Michael says.

"Jessie just threatened me with a knife!" he says, and I'm pulled away from trying to remember that dream. My mouth drops. Mother looks at me.

"Not even," I say, and Mother looks back at Keith, her expression a question mark.

"Well, not physically, but she looked at the knives and then at me," he explains weakly. Mother and I roll our eyes

6

in unison. She leaves, and from the dining room I hear the ring of jangling keys. "Let's go!" she calls, and we're out.

On the way to school, Keith and his whiny snot-nosed friends sit in the back seat and snicker while I try to piece together the dream. A ghost dream, but not a ghost . . . I'm lost in thought when suddenly the vision of two large black eyes swims into my brain, a remembrance not only from a dream but from life! The fragments fall into place, and I remember my granddaughter, and how I thought she was an alien, and how she told me there wasn't such a thing but that she was a human being from the future. And she warned me about something . . . what was it? Right. She warned me about Jimmy. And then she touched me before she vanished . . . wow, that dream seems too real. I'm really freaked but trying to stay cool as Mother speeds toward the parking lot at our school, while other moms glare at her recklessness. She stops the minivan with a screeching halt alongside Hollywood High's Sheik Territory mural. I get out of the car absently and touch the spot on my arm where The Granddaughter touched me. Keith is getting out of the car and he pokes me hard as he passes.

"Did 'oo get an owie?" he mimics in a baby voice as he and his freshman cronies walk on. I glance down at my arm. There are three long chevron-shaped silvery purple welts there, the same shape as The Granddaughter's fingers. I stare at the marks, astonished, as Mother yells, "close the door, Jessie! I'm late!"

I'm still standing there staring at the welts long after she's driven off.

Chapter Two

With The Granddaughter on my mind I forget to be careful on my way to class. Molly Johnston, who was once my best friend and is now my worst nightmare, shoves me, and my unzipped backpack goes flying, my books and homework sliding out onto to the sidewalk in front of the school. Her bimbo friends laugh as I bend over and begin shuffling papers into a pile.

"Ooh, sorry about that Jess. Don't kill yourself over it."

I remember what Michael says about counting to ten to control my deepening anger as I shoulder my backpack. One, two, three . . . my homework is covered in chalky white grime from the shoe bottoms of the entire Hollywood High population . . . four, five, six, seven . . . I grit my teeth and taste dirt as I wipe it off and shove my papers back into the notebook . . . eight, nine, ten . . .

"Oh, hi Moll. Klutz much?" I ask sweetly. Molly's posse, the same girls we both went to Girl Scout camp with years ago, giggle. Molly turns as red as her hair. I am calmer now, and I need to remember to tell my shrink Michael about this little victory: Here my arch nemesis and the most popular girl in school just got in my face, and I let it slide. I glare at her, wondering how it's possible that she could have been my friend once, and how can she still be friends with my boyfriend? The people at this school are crazier than the ones in the mental ward I lived in last year.

"Be careful, Jess," Molly says in a fakey-friendly way. "Jimmy doesn't want to date a girl who embarrasses herself in front of everybody."

"I'm not embarrassed," I say as I zip up my backpack.

"You should be," she whispers, and she brushes her fingertips across the faded scars on my left wrist. She and her best buddy Cristabelle Jenners, the bitch who turned Molly against me in the eighth grade, whisper as they slither away. I cringe but hold in the outburst that roils inside of me. Jimmy comes to the rescue, sweeping his arm across my middle.

"Hey babe," he says. He holds me up as I'm about to crumble and I feel relief. "I saw that whole thing. Molly's such a bitch."

"Can't you do anything about them?" I ask uselessly, but I know the rules even before he shakes his head. Jimmy's a jock, dating "The Freak" on campus (me). The only girl with dyed black hair and attempted suicide scars. And while I used to be a part of their group until our last year of middle school, when our dance classes turned into gagglefest cheerleading squads, and I thought it was lame and said so, then I became The Target. Now the cheerleading and jock crowd think I'm just a phase Jimmy's going through, and I can tell they're just waiting for me to disappear. But this time, I won't disappear. I smile up at Jimmy. He kisses me

9

slowly on the lips as the bell rings. My nightmare of a morning melts away. We go our own ways, me to science, and him to social studies, and I realize that in the confusion I forgot to tell him about The Granddaughter and show him the welts on my upper arm. When I put on my jacket in biology class I notice the marks are fading and hard to make out.

My shrink Michael is wearing his usual geeky Bill Cosby-inspired sweater, and once again I wonder who does his shopping. I suspect his mother but I've got more pressing issues at hand as I sit in his office after school. Coming here twice a week is the only way the school would take me back after what happened last spring.

"She did it on purpose," I mutter, and Michael nods knowingly. "But I counted to ten. I didn't get pissed off, I mean, lose my temper, or turn on myself. Just like you ordered."

"We have discussed the strong feelings Molly has about you regarding the person you've become, and how she cannot disassociate herself from you and it frightens her, so she acts out violently against you. Knowing that, how do you feel about maintaining control?" Michael asks in that light monotone way of his that, by now, feels really comforting.

I pause. Michael's trained me not to answer a question without thinking it through.

"I feel like I wish I'd hit her, because if I could just hit her once, she'd probably leave me alone and then I wouldn't have a problem." The honest answer.

Michael's disappointed by it, I can tell. He breathes in this nasally way when he's disappointed. When he's pleased, he licks his lips.

10

"Well, maybe that would solve that small portion of the problem. But you'd have a bigger problem, ultimately, wouldn't you? You'd be in trouble with the school, probably get detention or suspended, and then you'd have a lot of people angry with you."

"A lot of people are already angry with me," I say.

"Let's talk about that, then. What makes you feel as if people are angry with you?"

It's like a game we play, I think. I say this, you say that, I say this until I say the thing you want me to say, and then we stop, until next time. I'm a little tired so I try to think of something to say that he wants me to say.

"Well, aren't they angry, Michael? Didn't I break all the rules by trying to leave everything behind? It's like I ditched class and they all had to stay, and they're jealous. They didn't want to get left behind. They're curious, you know, but not brave enough to try it or anything like that. So they're mad at me. They can't relate to me any more because I broke the rules of the game."

There, I think. Chew on that for awhile. Michael licks his lips. I suppress my smile.

"So you think that people are angry with you because you made a move--trying to kill yourself--that they only wish they could make? Is that your feeling?" The monotone raises slightly at the end, and I know the session is nearly over. "And you relate suicide with ditching a class . . . that's a fascinating perspective, Jessie. And a very real response to your past history. I appreciate it when you share with me on that level. Your feelings about how others view you may be valid, Jessie, but that doesn't mean that their feelings are accurately portraying you. You are not their feelings. You are your own person. You don't need to get caught up in other people's opinions of you."

11

"I know," I say, and I mean it but I'm bored with the Michael Game now. What I really want to say is that I was visited by an alien last night, Michael, only she wasn't really an alien but my great-great-great-great-great infinity time-traveling granddaughter from eons in the future! And there really are no aliens, just these humanoids from her time, and I'm some sort of genetic marker for this future race of humans and my relationship with Jimmy Becker has something to do with it, isn't that beyond cool? But I know, by now, exactly what will and won't get me thrown back into the Not-So-Funny-Farm. I shut down, pull my energy inward. Michael studies me a moment and recognizes that it's time to stop.

"That's enough for today, Jessie. Except before we go I want to talk to you more about your brother . . . that look you gave the knives this morning was an immature step backward, don't you agree?"

"Mother called you?"

"Yes, as I have asked her to do when you regress to this level. However your standing up to Molly Johnston was a step forward, and I applaud you. These are all the tiny steps toward recovery, Jessie. I'm proud of you."

Michael gives me his usual little impersonal sideways shoulder squeeze, and pats me on the arm, right where The Granddaughter touched me. The spot burns a bit after he touches it but I still have my hoodie on so I can't tell if the welts are there. I'm tempted to check but decide it would be too hard to explain if they are there.

"I'll see you at our next scheduled appointment, then," Michael says and I pick up my backpack and leave. I rush to the bathroom at the end of the hallway. Once inside I slip my jacket off my shoulder. The welts are there, and I'm surprised. They look even more glowy than before. I'm even more surprised when I look in the mirror, and there beyond my tired face and messy *Ebony-Midnight Number Three* hair stands The Granddaughter, shimmering in that wavy blue way and looking down on me with the wisdom of the ages shining in her huge black eyes. I turn around and there is no one there, no tall alien-like being standing behind me with those knowing eyes, but when I look in the bathroom mirror again I see that blue sparkling light that I saw the night before when The Granddaughter disappeared, and suddenly I feel woozy. The floor beneath me is rubbery and coming closer, closer. I surrender to it.

Chapter Three

"Jessie, wake up now," I hear, and I'm back in Michael's office. He looks concerned as his secretary fans me with one of the reception room magazines. I stare at the white ceiling and it seems far away, but the cool green walls envelop me like a forest, like a breath of nature. I'm glad of the familiar surroundings, of leather couch, tapestry chairs, and that desk Michael always sits behind. Things here make sense. Like I'm home, but not.

"Good girl, Jessie. Come back to us. You fainted." Michael looks to Marjorie, the receptionist with the purple painted fingernails and matching lipstick. "Thanks, Marj. I've got it from here."

Michael helps me onto the sofa, which I've never actually sat on before. I always choose the left chair. The couch feels smooth and cool under me and I'm suddenly tired. I want to lie down, so I do.

"Are you all right?" Michael asks, his voice not the usual monotone.

"I'll be okay. I didn't eat much lunch today, and forgot to eat my snack after school."

"Do you have something to eat?"

I nod and point at my backpack on the floor. Michael hands it to me and I take out a slightly bruised apple from two days ago. I eat it lying down, staring at the way the overhead lights reflect in its red peel.

"Tell me about what's happening here," Michael says.

"What," I say. Not a question. Let him tell me something.

"You're different today. Tell me why. No bullshit."

I sigh. I sit up. I chew. I stare at Michael. He stares back.

"I'm seeing something . . ." I say. Chewing again. Swallowing. Apples are so sweet.

"Seeing . . . something? Not someone?" he asks.

"Something, someone. I'm not sure. It's a . . . thing. A person, I guess. Someone."

"Who?"

I pause. I can't tell him what I know, what The Granddaughter has shared. Somehow it seems like a secret. But I can't lie, either. I don't lie to Michael, not really. I play the game we play, but I don't lie. And who else can I talk to about The Granddaughter?

"It's a woman, I think. But not really. She's tall and gray and has big eyes and can . . . shimmer, you know, disappear and reappear, in and out of my room. She looks like an alien. I saw her last night. And just now. She's like a visitor or something. She touched me and it left a mark."

I place my hand over the area The Granddaughter touched. Michael looks at me, at my arm, back into my eyes.

15

As if I am some delicate instrument with important survival instructions but I must be read just right, or something will self-destruct. Probably me.

"Are you afraid?" he asks.

"Um . . . no. Well, at first, last night, but I didn't pass out because I was afraid. I just . . . " I can't explain it. The Granddaughter takes something from me when she comes to me, like she steals a piece of my soul away. I shrug.

"Did she talk to you?"

"Last night she told me some stuff."

"What stuff?"

"Just, stuff. She warned me about Jimmy, weirdly enough."

"I see."

Michael makes a note in my file, and I realize I led him right to an assumption. I'm having problems with Jimmy now, in Michael's mind. I must want to leave/change/upgrade/something that relationship. It's an issue I clearly haven't explored, so I'm seeing silver aliens in my bedroom until I get to the bottom of it. How brilliant the teenage mind is! Michael must surely be pleased with his new discovery.

"You didn't tell me earlier," Michael says, switching tacks.

"I thought it was just a dream, until I saw her shimmering again in the bathroom."

"Just now," Michael says.

"Yes, just now."

Michael writes again. I'm getting that nagging feeling I got right after I slashed my wrist last spring, when my cuts were healing but my mind was doubtful. I'd felt so right in doing it then, and was a little disappointed my dad found me in time but hey, whatever, I made it. I lived. But the whole world is still treating me as if I were the alien, an unknowable thing that can't be touched or trusted and can never fit in, and people won't look me in the eyes anymore, and just for awhile, before I realized most people are assholes who will never get it, I wondered. This nagging, creeping doubt kept coming to me: Was I really wrong for doing what I did? Am I nuts? Am I the bad one here, even though it's my life? Everyone but Dad treated me like I was the alien. Mother is still a mess and while I was in the hospital she would only come and say hello and pat my arm and then wait in the hall while Dad talked to me and told me about his latest gaffer gig on the movie set and he'd tell me about the stars and how they acted, and mostly they were okay, he said, but sometimes they'd be jerks and he'd tell me about that too.

"Are you --seeing -- the alien now?" Michael asks. I come out of my daze, feeling anger welling up in me. *Quit treating me like a moron, Michael.*

"No."

Michael writes again, and I put down my apple and unzip my hoodie. The welts are on my upper arm, lightly glowing. I triumphantly show them to Michael.

"She left these, last night, if you don't believe me," I say.

Michael gets up and walks over to me. He reaches toward my upper arm but hesitates and doesn't touch the welts.

"Does it hurt?" he asks in a dry voice.

I shake my head, wondering if he believes me. But there's something in his eyes, something beyond his believing me or not, something more like suspicion. I cover my arms by pulling up my jacket. Michael sits back down.

"I don't know what's happening," I say, my confidence shattered. "Do you think I really am being abducted by aliens or something?"

"We'll look into it, Jessie. Try not to worry about it. I've read about things like this . . . "

"About alien abductions?"

"About alien abductions and how they relate to mental wellness," Michael says stiffly. I nod dumbly as I usually do when Michael says inane things like that. But I can kind of put together what it means . . . he thinks I'm crazy and that I think I'm being abducted by aliens. Great. But I won't give The Granddaughter up, not to him.

"Um . . . can I go home? Mother worries if I miss the bus."

"Yes, we are a bit behind schedule today. And I'm glad to hear that you're concerned about your mother's feelings. Go ahead . . . are you sure you're all right? I can arrange for a ride."

"I'm good. The apple helped." I get my backpack and head out, a usual act but everything feels different, like Michael and I just went on a trip together and didn't get along. I should stay and fix things with him but I'm still dizzy and not ready to play the game. I just want to go and curl up in my bed and sleep, something Michael told Mother she should let me do. Michael believes teens need more sleep than anyone else, even as much as babies, thank God for me. I'm always so damn tired.

I close my eyes and try to close out the sound on Santa Monica Boulevard as I wait for the bus. Mother is at work till six or seven, and her assistant is probably driving my brother to wherever it is he goes after school. There's no one really waiting for me at home. It takes twenty minutes to get to my stop, but within thirty minutes I'm lying on my bed

18

watching the late afternoon sun hit my wall, watching patterns of leaf shadows dance in a chaotic silent way across the ecru paint. My eyes grow tired, and finally I'm able to drift away from my mind again, my favorite place to be.

Chapter Four

It's dark when I open my eyes, and for a moment I struggle to remember where I am: at home, in my bed, in my own room. It was that way a lot after I tried to off myself, where I'd wake up and for a moment forget about everything, forget about all that emotion that seemed to float just beyond where I could touch it. Forget about that look in Mother's eyes, or the way my brother avoided me and wouldn't talk to me, and forget the fact that my dad had been the one to find me, the one who called 911. All of that disappears in that instant between awake and sleep, consciousness and dreaming. A flash of light in the corner of my room catches my eye, and I realize I'm not alone.

"What are you doing here?" I can just make out Jimmy's form in my desk chair. He's slouched, playing with that St. Christopher's medal he always wears around his neck.

Which is a good thing, because St. Christopher is the patron saint of travelers, and Jimmy for sure is on a long strange trip, with me as his girlfriend. He moves his fingers to make the medal reflect the street light outside my window, then flicks the lightbeam around the room with a twist of hand. He aims it to the top of my bookcase and illuminates my Buffy the Vampire DVD collection and on the faces of my pewter ballet trophy figures. The chiseled dancers' features stare blankly down on us.

"Hey, sleepyhead," Jimmy says, coming over to me. He folds back the bright pink and green Anthropologie Hothouse Floral comforter on my bed and climbs in beside me and hugs me, and I melt into him the way I always do. He smells so good I can barely stand it. I just want to curl up next to him and stay that way, mushed together for days. But Mother doesn't even want him in my room, let alone for an eternity sleep over. It's hard to pull myself away from him. He sits me up and turns on the lamp beside my bed.

"You're all rumply," he says. "You look so damn cute."

"What time is it?" I ask.

"7:30, Friday night. No homework, and . . . date night."

I grin up at him and he tousles my hair. My insides are singing with happiness because he's here.

"How long have you been in my room?"

"You're hard to find, Jess. I've looked everywhere for you, then I remembered the nap thing, how you like to nap in the late afternoon. So I snuck in and just chilled, watching you sleep. You look like a princess lying there. The sunlight covered you at sunset. You were glowing. It was really cool."

At first I can't believe Jimmy was watching me sleep, but then I picture myself watching him sleep and I realize I could do it endlessly so I get it.

21

Jimmy kisses me and I wonder if my breath stinks as bad as I think it does but he doesn't seem to mind. I don't even know if my mother and brother are home so I'm a little distracted. This would look so bad if we got walked in on, like it was planned and not just some innocent thing. As we kiss, I wish we didn't have to go through the motions of him climbing back out my window, going to the front door, and waiting for me to get ready for my "date" for the sake of my family. I wish it could just be us, with no distractions, nothing to take us away from that feeling I get when I'm with Jimmy. But now my creepy brother is making noises in the hall and we know our time is limited. Jimmy kisses me once more and climbs out my window onto the carport roof. I snap on the light and hurriedly throw on something not-too-filthy to wear and brush my teeth, because I suspect my date will be arriving any minute. Don't want to make him wait.

Everyone at the party ignores me, which is a good thing, because for awhile they used to just talk about me behind my back. I would look over and see them pointing and whispering about me as if I couldn't see what they were doing. At least this ignoring thing is a more decent way to dis me. I just follow Jimmy around as he socializes from one end of the large garage rec room to the other. I sip Vanilla Coke® from a red plastic cup and breathe into it to quell the stink of beer and cigarettes, happy when Jimmy puts his arm around me and squeezes me in the rear. I'm wearing my lowest jeans, a bunch of tank tops layered into a rainbow of colors at my hips (the underneath ones are the dirtiest), and my black Converse while the rest of them are mini-skirted and high-heeled. Again, who are these people?

Screw them: I'm his, they like him, so they have to deal with me. Tough shit if they have a problem with that.

After the third conversation about that touchdown last month at the homecoming game, I'm bored. I want Jimmy all to myself, in the back seat of his car. Listening to music and kissing him, maybe more. I start rubbing his lower back, and he loses the thread of his conversation as he talks. I like being able to control him while he's with me with just a touch.

"See you guys later," Jimmy says with a wink and we leave the jocks and cheerleaders and the stupid party behind. As we walk down the driveway toward the street, the cool night air fills my lungs and we're free. Ourselves again.

"Let's take a drive," Jimmy says as we walk toward his ghetto convertible. I laugh as he picks me up and lifts me over the broken passenger door through the window and settles me into the front seat, something I secretly love. It's so gentlemanly, forget the women's movement. Soon we're zipping up the dark canyon roads out past the mansions to the vacant area where everyone parks and parties on Friday nights. It's crowded already, duh. But we find a spot sort of away from the others and Jimmy puts on my favorite oldie Avril Lavigne CD. It's times like this when I can really be myself, free of that other crap that's always messing with my life: the family-in-crisis shit that we use to identify ourselves to the world. I don't want to be that anymore. Can't my family see, it's over? We can be okay if they'd just let go and move on.

We sit together and look at the lights of Los Angeles below us, a dizzying glowing grid squashed by an infinite stripe of black (the Pacific), topped by mottled gray (the nighttime clouded sky on the horizon). Jimmy gets out and arranges the rag top so it can be put down. He loves his '65 Dodge Coronet that his dad gave him for his sixteenth birthday . . . sometimes I think of it as his other girlfriend. He finds a striped blanket in his trunk and hops back in the front seat, covering us and breathing into his cold hands. He puts his hands under my shirts to warm them and starts kissing me. I lean into him and our lips mosh for awhile. We break away, hot and restless, but it always comes to this point. I want to have sex with him, but not here. Not yet. Not at some lame Lover's Lane overlooking the whole city in suburbia. And I know I shouldn't anyway. Michael has pretty much assured me that if I start having a "more adult relationship" with Jimmy than I'm ready for in my "weakened psychological state" that it might "hinder my emotional growth and recovery." Whatever, Michael. I just want to have fun, but how I can have a good time with words like that hanging over my head? Jimmy sifts through the CDs using his key chain light, trying to act as if he's not annoyed with the lack of action.

"Did you enjoy the party?" he asks mildly, hooking up his iPod to the car speakers. Throbbing dubstep fills the air.

"At least they weren't talking about me behind my back this time," I say, turning down the music.

"They probably did after we left, but don't sweat it Jess. I'm here." Jimmy puts his arm around me again. His hands start to wander toward my crotch.

"You're probably right," I say, leaning against him, and I put his hand on my thigh and hold it still. I think suddenly about The Granddaughter. What's up with that? Here's the most amazing guy, the best thing that's ever happened to me in my whole life, and some weird-ass-looking alien freak from the future is telling me not to date him anymore? I don't think so.

24

"The weirdest thing happened to me last night," I say gamely.

"Hmmmm?" He's wriggling his fingers under my shirts again.

"I had this dream, only I swear it wasn't a dream . . . it was just like it really happened. This woman from the future visited me and said she was . . . my offspring, like my great-great-great-quadmillion-drillion granddaughter and that I was a . . . a genetic marker and that, like, the fate of all evolution of the human species was in my hands. That I was the key to it. Genetically."

Jimmy laughs and pulls me in tighter. "That's what I love about you, Jess. You're completely whacked, but in a really cool way."

I'm a little offended but in a way relieved that he doesn't take The Granddaughter seriously. If he did, then I'd eventually probably tell him what she said about him, that he was the end of the genetic future. A no-no boy. Jimmy Becker, Hollywood High's senior class Best Athlete, A.K.A. The End of Civilization As We Know It.

I snuggle closer to Jimmy, glad to drop it and just hang out.

Chapter Five

"You told him." The Granddaughter hovers in the center of my room in the middle of the night, and her eyes suck me in like tarry pools.

"Don't worry, he didn't believe me," I say, trying to get my bearings. It's not that I don't expect her to come to me by now, but when she does it still catches me off guard. She's so hard to talk to. She steals my thoughts, breathes them in. I sit up, trying to feel taller in my cluttered bedroom.

"Jimmy Becker. You love him," The Granddaughter says, but I shrug.

"So?"

"And he returns this love to you?"

What a question! Who is this . . . *thing* that wants so much from me? Not one person, not even Michael, asks me questions that turn my stomach into a pit of wrestling alligators. But there is something about The Granddaughter that makes me think about things, stuff I usually don't want

26

to think about. Like why the hell Jimmy Becker, one of the most popular jocks in school, is with me. Me, Jessie Allen, with a guy that most of the other girl-droids in my school drool over. And he loves me. Or does he?

"Does he?" repeats The Granddaughter with her thoughts, and for the first time I realize she knows me all the way through. She's heard everything I've ever thought about her. She is me, in a way. More than Michael, Jimmy, or Dad. The thought feeds on my mind and chaos erupts. I feel faint.

"I don't know," I admit, and realize she knows I don't know. That's exactly why she's asking, to make me think about it. Then I realize further, that she now knows that I not only don't know if Jimmy loves me, but that I now know she knows that I know that's why she's asking me. I have to lean my head back on the pillow. I feel as if an enormous wave just swallowed me and I forgot to take a breath first.

"It's something you must consider," The Granddaughter says, and I feel a release from the flooding of thoughts. I float to the surface of her words that form in my head.

"There are many things you must consider. I am not here to tell you what to do, Jessica, but to help you define your thoughts as you make your own choices. I am a sounding board. I will reflect back to you what thoughts you send to me."

Now I know why I'm dizzy. I'm being double-thoughted. I want to laugh at the silliness of that but it's not funny. Why is Jimmy Becker my boyfriend?

"Was he there before you attempted to take your own life?" The Granddaughter asks.

"No . . ." I say, and realize I don't really need to speak. She can hear me just fine. She's in my friggin' head, after all. No, I think. In fact, Jimmy Becker wouldn't give me the time

27

of day last year until after I came back from my stay in the hospital. To me he was just this cute jock that all of my ex-friends latched onto when he started HH his sophomore year. Then suddenly while I was in the library all those PE exempt days literally trying to get my life back last spring, he saunters in with this broken collar bone and parks himself right next to me. His first words to me were, so you're the girl who tried to kill herself. Jessie Allen. I said yes and he smiled and whispered under his breath, cool. Just like that. Cool. Like he got it, the whole thing, why I did it, and I didn't even have to say one word.

You said yes, The Granddaughter reminds me. Yes to Jimmy Becker.

He understands me. The only one in this whole damn mess of my life who understands I'm not depressed or any of those labels Michael wants to put on it, that it was like a game, a competition to see if I could win. And I did it. I won Death. I went there and back and I made it.

That makes you feel superior, The Granddaughter tells me.

In a way I am superior. Sort of like super-human, and Jimmy sees that in me. That's why we're together.

I see, The Granddaughter says mentally.

Clarity is a beautiful white light, I realize. It brings together your whole world and cements it into place. For the first time, I don't have any doubts about what Jimmy sees in me. And ironically, The Granddaughter, the one whose very future supposedly rides on my relationship with Jimmy, has given me that clarity. Who the hell would have thought.

"Jess?" I hear Dad's voice in the hallway, and my heart races as The Granddaughter shimmers away when he opens the door. He looks at the spot where she was hovering moments before and rubs his eyes. The hall light illuminates me on the bed.

"Dad!" I call, and he comes in and sits on my bed and holds me close to him. I breathe him in . . . sweaty T-shirt, and that weird lighting equipment metallic smell that sinks into his pores when he's been working.

"I thought I saw a light in your room. What are you doing up?"

"I don't know, I think I was having a nightmare," I say, holding Dad's calloused hand. "How's the set?"

"Good, the usual grind, sweetums. We just wrapped yesterday, I'm home for awhile now, the boys and I just put up our equipment in the warehouse. My next job doesn't start until the middle of next month."

"Mother will be glad," I say. "So am I. Who did you see this time?"

"Taylor Lautner."

"You did not!"

"I did, at the studio lot, not in Canada." Dad goes on, filling my head with the names of the celebrities he sees every day as he works as a gaffer, the wizard who lights up the scenes and literally makes the stars shine down from the night sky.

Chapter Six

Dad and I are horsing around in the kitchen, playing *en garde* with plastic spatulas. I jump *sur les pointes* to avoid a swat across my thigh and he smiles. We love to sword fight. Dad learned how once on a set. At the Renaissance Faire every year Dad and Keith and I dress up and go with wooden swords and take on all the knights there. We look really cool cuz Dad got a hold of costumes from a movie he worked on three years ago so our costumes are as good as the fair workers. Mother used to braid my hair in a Renaissance-y way, but last year we didn't go because I was in the whack-job hospital, and my hair is short and black now. No more girly braids.

Mother walks in and eyes us in a suspicious way.

"Greg," Mother says, and Dad stops in mid-jab, his spatula falling limp in his hand.

"*En garde*, m'lady," Dad says to her in his best British accent, and he rushes over to Mother and starts poking at her with the spatula. He hugs her from behind and keeps poking her in the ribs and she laughs, and it's the first time I've seen her smile since the last time he was home. I smile but wish he were still playing with me. Keith the Wretched Brother walks in and sees fun happening without him. He lunges for Dad, his hair a mess from his usual nighttime tossings.

"Dad!" he says, jumping on his back. His arms go around Dad's neck and Dad keeps holding onto Mother, but now he's trying to whack Keith on the head with the spatula, and they've become a writhing laughing human ball.

"I didn't know you were home," Keith says, jumping down off of Dad's back. He's almost as big as Dad and I can see relief in Dad's face. Mother straightens her hair and robe and pours herself some coffee. I haven't seen her in anything but work clothes forever. Dad jabs Keith in the ribs with the spatula next.

"Here, freak," I say, tossing my scraper to him so he can swordfight. He catches it, game on.

"Be nice to your brother, "Mother mutters.

"I am being nice. I gave him a weapon, didn't I?" I sip my coffee.

Mother stares at me in this way I don't get. It reminds me of The Granddaughter as her eyes become those same dark pools, pools of I-Don't-Know-What. Not anger, not love, not understanding , but somehow a combination of all three, but with hesitation mixed in. There's something else in there, a darkness. Pain? I don't know. It makes me uncomfortable the way she stares.

Keith and Dad collide into us and we barely save our coffees to the counter. I become a damsel in distress and flee

31

as Mother becomes a trapped Rapunzel on the edge of the kitchen sink. She smacks them with an oven mitt as they swordfight beneath her.

"Stop, you cads! Stop!" she squeals as Dad throws her over his shoulder. The spatula falls to the floor and he runs through the swinging kitchen door with her. The kitchen falls quiet as the energy of action settles away into the corners of the room. We hear the pounding of Dad's heavy feet on the stairs and Mother's laughter far away.

"Lost the maiden fair and square to that one," Keith says, picking up the spatula and putting it in the sink. He opens the fridge and pulls up some orange juice. I look at the clock. Good thing it's not a school day or we'd be late.

Kara Slauson sits across from me at Starbucks. I haven't seen her except on Skype since last year, when we were in the head-case hospital together, but we Facebook and text each other a lot now that she got out of her latest hospital stay, so she wanted to see me. She has tattoos up her arms now to hide the scars from her cutting problem and her suicide attempt. They look like blue and black flames and you can't tell her arms used to resemble nicked up ice at a skating rink after a public session.

"I can't believe you're sitting here. It's so weird. I mean, we're dressed in real clothes, out in public, no doctors around."

"I still have plenty of doctors," Kara says with a shrug. "Now I just go and visit them, on my schedule."

I nod, thinking of Michael. We aren't so free yet, she's right. I sip my caramel latte and look around. Sunday--there are no classmates of mine here to see me talking with the freaky tattooed girl. I'm a little disappointed.

"So how's life in the real world, Jess? Are you the school zombie too? The one who came back from the dead?"

"Yeah . . . sort of. But since I hooked up with Jimmy, he's saving me right now. I hope you can meet him soon. I told you he's a jock, you know, B.M.O.C., my dad calls him that. Big Man On Campus. People don't mess with me too much cuz they know I'm with him. Well, except some wretched cheerleaders but what do you expect."

"Wow, that sounds almost tolerable. The only guy I've even dated was some college guy who also tried to kill himself in high school. He was so depressing I dumped him." Kara smiles, pushing her overly-dyed red and black streaked hair behind her ear. "What a loser."

"He didn't get you?" I ask, breaking off a piece of my crumble cake, pinching it together with my fingers so it won't fall apart all over my lap.

"No, he was a head-case. Depressed, paranoid . . . had one of those secret government conspiracy things going on."

"Well, those are usually true," I say, making my eyes roll around in a crazy way. Kara smiles and eats her zucchini cake and sips her iced chai latte.

"He wasn't like us. . ." Kara's cell rings and she holds up a black-fingernailed hand and answers. We really are two groups of people, us suicide attempters. There are psychos, the ones who don't see it as a game but as a way to leave the planet, hurt everyone they ever loved, and leave a bitter spot in their absence. Kara and I aren't that way. We are more like dare devils, risk takers, people who want to explore the edge of this reality but we made it back. Not that we cared if we did or didn't come back. Going there at all, touching that line made us special. Kara is the only person in my life who really gets that. She's a senior like Jimmy; soon she'll be free to live her life and get beyond the whole

33

high school suicide attempt label. As we sit on the usual Starbucks-beige couch, I find myself wishing that I only had a few months left of school as Kara texts someone and then snaps her phone shut.

"My sister needs money, what else is new. Sorry." She gives me an ironic look. "So you're doing okay?"

"I'm good, I'm still seeing my therapist. It's mandatory, part of the school's deal to let me back in. But it's just a lie. There's some stuff I can barely tell him."

I halt, wanting to tell her about The Granddaughter. I know she'd think it was cool, but maybe later on she'd tell someone, "Oh Jessie? She's okay but she's psycho now. She's seeing time travelers from the future or some weird shit . . ."

"I hear you," Kara says, her hands dancing in front of her. "My last head shrinker was nuttier than I ever was! You know what his hobby is? Taxidermy! You know, making dead animals look lifelike? How creepy, don't you think? I asked him about it and he told me there's power in bringing things back to a new form after death, and that's why most of his patients are suiciders! So I'm like some roadkill on the freeway to him, right? Let's see if we can make this dead thing whole again! How nasty is that?"

"Nasty." I shudder, glad Michael is at least human. I've had a lot of weird-ass doctors; he could be worse.

"I'm with Marsha now, my new shrink. She's cool. She's helping me with 'my issues.'"

"Like what?" I ask, not really paying attention as I scan the aromatic coffee house for my high school peers.

"Well, my mom split, remember?"

I had forgotten but I nod, refocusing on Kara.

"My dad is starting to visit me at my Grandma's. We're talking about giving it another go. He's tried to get me back into the regular school. . . your school . . . but I'm stuck at continuation for now. Grandma's cool, she's the only one treating me like I won't break. She's pretty strict, actually. She calls her way of dealing with me 'snapping me back into shape.' At first it really pissed me off but now I sort of appreciate the fact that she's organized. My dad takes me to my appointments and stuff. How 'bout you?"

"Dad's home, he's in between jobs, which is good. He's cool, like nothing happened. But my mother. . ." I hesitate. What is going on with her? I think of the discombobulated way we start each day with missing keys, dirty laundry, and yelling about being late, but she's not mean. She's distant. Like an island far off on the horizon that I can see, that I want to touch and experience and understand, but it's too far to swim. I know I can't make it. The journey itself will kill me.

"Your mom?" Kara asks, pulling me away from my lost thoughts as the whirring of the cappuccino machine hums in the background.

"It's like she's not there," I say. "She's . . ."

"A cold fish." Kara says, finishing my sentence and her drink. Her words are different from the ones that I would use but there it is, the essence of Mother. My cold fish.

"Probably why you tried to dump yourself in the first place," Kara observes. I just stare as she rattles the ice in the bottom of her cup while sucking the last sip of chai loudly through her green straw.

Chapter Seven

Again with the waking me up in the middle of the night. The room hums with that peculiar buzz as The Granddaughter shimmers before me.

"Hi," I say, sitting up and rubbing my eyes. I like the way the whole room is lit up by her presence.

"Hello, Jessica, how is your life this evening?"

"Good," I reply, ignoring her weird syntax. "Daddy's home, so things are normal again." Even as I say it, I realize it's not true, just something our family says when Dad's not working and he's in town. Things haven't been normal since last spring when everything changed because of one stupid night when I was feeling crazy and invincible. Just one night.

"One night can change everything," The Granddaughter says, and I remember she's reading my mind. Okay, fine, read my mind. I talk anyway because telepathically communicating with her kind of freaks me out.

"It's over, doesn't anyone get it? I lived, I didn't die. How much time does it take to get over it?" I wonder what Michael's answer to that question would be.

"You must find your own answers, Jessica. The answers to your life don't live in others. And remember, there's no such thing as time. Not really. It is a conventional, man-made concept."

"You said that before. That there is no time, but you wouldn't talk about it then. Why are you talking about it now?"

"I had to be certain I would not disrupt any waves from this Consciousness, this Reality, as you call it. From this Time, if you insist on calling it that. I have been assured it is safe for me to discuss almost anything with you. Others perceive you as fragile. If you were to tell all of your significant others of me, it has been calculated that there is a 92.4% chance that you would not be believed, as Early Humanoids of your lifespace are not very evolved."

I stare, my mouth hanging open, until I remember to close it. Does she know she's being rude? Does she care?

"I am an Early Humanoid!" I reply sarcastically, finding myself thinking reprimanding and disturbingly mothering thoughts about her behavior. I push the feeling away, wondering if she thinks I'm insane.

"I do not believe that you are mentally incapacitated, Jessica. Do not assume that is my thought of you. I am from a different construct, and my construct is more advanced than yours so I must reflect the information I have to share with you in a way for you to understand. It is like speaking two languages at once. You might say that I am translating this information to you so you will understand. Where I am from, communication is a simple, singular and universal thing, and all understanding is one with all living beings, including plants and single-celled organisms. Here I must fragment what I know just to communicate with humanoids of your development. Do you realize how difficult it is for me to be here speaking with you, Jessica? It takes a great deal of focused concentration."

Now I'm really insulted. "Why are you here?" I ask. "How come you keep coming back? You already warned me about Jimmy! Is there something else you've forgotten to tell me, like that I'm supposed to kill my parents in my sleep or something?"

I forget to keep my voice low and remember my parents asleep down the hall. I hope they didn't hear that. I cough to cover my words.

"I see you're displaying humor. Or is it sarcasm? I have never been able to differentiate the two." She speaks so Spock-like I'm beginning to feel like I'm losing it, as if she isn't real and this is just a bad drug trip of some kind. Except for the hospital meds I've never taken drugs, but I'm thinking it must be something like this, only freakier.

She must sense my feelings because she tells me, "I am here because you make a difference, Jessica. You are one of the keys to a future generation of people who will essentially save this planet and along that path develop into a more cognizant being, a being one with the universe much as I am. The being that the people of your Time call aliens."

I suck in my breath, not really wanting to hear anymore. Don't they kill people with this kind of classified information? I feel like covering my ears with my hands and singing la-la-la to drown out her voice but she hurries on.

"I am a human of the future, Jessica, as I have explained. My people are Earthlings, or were once born of this planet called Earth. But Jimmy Becker is not of the bloodline and DNA needed to sustain the race of humankind. I tell you this catastrophic news and your response is to go on an amusement with him . . . a 'date.' I fail to understand your logic."

Logic, I think. Logic? I'm a sixteen year old with a shimmery blue and silver talking alien in my bedroom and she wants to know why I'm not being logical? I almost want to laugh and a small smile indents her chevron mouth. Right then I realize, I don't want to believe in her. How can I have anything whatever to do with the future? I'm barely here myself. I look at the indentation on my wrist where a razor blade once sliced through my skin and brought forth a bubbling red eruption, the last thing I remember seeing as I keeled over on the upstairs bathroom floor. Surgery has since hidden much of the mark deep inside my skin, but I know what the indentation is. I know what happened.

I glare up at her, defiant. Now she knows why I won't obey her ridiculous command. There's no way I can have any affect on the world whatsoever. She shimmers away without another word or thought, her blue effervescent light darker than usual.

I'm twisting my bandanna into a knot as I sit across from Michael. I'm sorry I told him. Michael senses something is wrong so he waits. With every second of his breath I can feel the knot loosening, the words ready to tumble out.

"I'm not crazy, if that's what you're thinking," I say forcefully. "Though she must think I'm crazy, cuz she said if I told anyone about her, there's like a 99.9% chance that no one would believe me anyway. Doesn't she have a clue she's being rude when she says shit like that?"

I watch Michael frantically flip through his notes. He lands on an informed page, and sits back in his seat, his calm self again.

"Yes, your . . . great-great-great-great et cetera granddaughter, from the future, is it? Go on. How does that make you feel when she says those things to you?"

I just want to smack him one, that's how I feel. Sometimes when I get up in the morning to pee, I hear Michael asking me that question: And how does that make you feel? It's his favorite line, and I usually can throw him a bone as he adds my feelings to his notes, but today I'm not playing this stupid Sims game anymore. Now that I'm doubting The Granddaughter, this is real creepy stuff, and Michael has to quit playing therapist and start *being* one.

"Why don't you tell me what I'm supposed to feel, Michael? Isn't that what we do? I say something, you get all sad and disappointed about it, I fix it, you say, now you're getting there Jessie, good girl Jessie, and then I go home?"

The words hang there, more anger in them than I realize. But it's not just Michael. It's The Granddaughter. I tossed and turned all last night after she left, wondering if I was crazy. Maybe I am nuts. Michael drops his pen and puts down his yellow writing tablet. He takes off his glasses, leans forward in his chair. Stares at me.

"Why don't you tell me what you really feel, Jessie, for once?" Michael challenges. The sweet gazelle of Michael has suddenly turned into a hungry lion. I feel myself pressing against the chair, trying to escape the pounce. It's too late.

Feelings burst to the surface in a sweaty rush of energy. I feel actual pain, I think. This question is giving me real pain. It's hard to breathe and I'm squirming all over the place. How do I feel? How do I feel? I feel like my head is going to explode if I see that weird alien chick one more time. I feel as if I'm losing my mind, aren't I just? I feel as if my life will never get back to normal, that Mother will never forgive me and Dad will never acknowledge what happened. I feel trapped by what I've done.

"Scared," I say in a tiny voice, realizing that this small word sums it up for me. This is who I really am. Hello, I'm Scared. What's your name?

"I feel scared about what I did," I say it louder this time, and I'm surprised. That's not what I thought I was feeling at all. I always thought I felt triumphant. What's Scared doing here, a part of me?

Michael rubs his eyes and bends his head forward and I'm trying to see his face, to make out the next move, but the game has crashed all around me. Besides, I don't need to see him. I know that Michael is the triumphant one, but his features have become a blur. I can't see anything but water, tears filling my own eyes, hot and wet as they careen down my face. Game over, and I am ruined.

Chapter Eight

I feel as if someone has turned me inside out and wrung me dry as I stare out the window of the city bus on my way home from Michael's office. I'm like a different person, a shy, meek version of myself. I have no tears left. Outside my window the streets of Hollywood are gritty and full of people driving in cars, walking in clusters, and waving their arms as they talk on cell phones. Beside me I overhear classical music from a businessman's iPod and the scene outside becomes suddenly hyper-real, like a music video. Boys in wool caps and low baggy jeans jive down the street, their basketball bouncing to the orchestral beat of pavement. People waiting for the bus cock their heads in synch with timpani as they hear the coughing diesel in the distance. A mom scurrying her kids across an intersection runs remarkably like a chicken in tempo with staccato piano.

There's so much life out there, life that has nothing to do with me. I watch and feel sad that I haven't noticed anything outside these windows in a long, long time.

The bus turns the corner on Santa Monica Boulevard toward the beginnings of suburbia, rows of older bungalows and untidy scraps of front lawn. Soon enough the lawns are greener, the homes restored, and I can feel my own neighborhood creeping up on me. Mother has always loved our house that she and Dad bought when they first got married. Then it was one and a half bedrooms and one bath. She told me once that Dad went out on a limb adding the second story in a bungalow town. It was still a short, squat, blendy kind of house, a compromise of aesthetics but with room for two kids. Yet somehow, even though they made room for us, I never felt as if there was room enough growing up. Not room for me, the weird one, the troubled kid with no clean underwear whose only solace was dance class, the only place I ever fit in until Molly and Cristabelle made even that too much torture to bear.

The bus passes streets that lead to the houses of kids I know, dead starlet's estates with elegant driveways and rambling guest quarters behind locked gates. Hollywood is a weird town, and even though it's the only place I've ever lived, still I feel that weirdness. Home is home but the rest of this neighborhood is like some movie set. As we near my stop I see some neighbors walking their gangly puppy and have a vague memory of an older dog. I remember Mother saying that the dog died and the family was devastated. She said they waited over a year to get the new puppy. I wonder how Mother knows these things about the people who live all around us and wonder what they know about me. I wish I could remember my neighbors' names. Did I ever know?

The bus goes past our street and I catch a glimpse of our house halfway down the block, all wood trim and yellow paint and those mailbox flowers Mother spends the weekends planting and watering and trimming while inside my laundry pile is reaching the ceiling and last year's Christmas boxes are still in the living room, stashed behind our couch, waiting for someone to put them into the crawl space above the hallway. Mother's home, her van's parked in the driveway. Keith's bike is parked by the front steps with his helmet and Rollerblades and skateboard cluttering up the walkway. The usual.

The bus stops on the next corner and I exit.

"Bye, Jessie," the bus driver says, and it startles me. I forgot that I used to know the black man with the high cheekbones. We used to talk sometimes. Isn't his name Ernest? I've been taking this bus for years to Beverly Hills to shop, to my ballet and tap lessons, back when my life was normal. I nod, my throat too raw to utter sound. I feel like I'm the one in a time warp. Did the last year even happen?

I walk slowly back down the sidewalk and turn left onto my block. I step over the skateboard and newspaper and I realize I don't want to see my family. I just want to go straight to my room and bury myself under blankets the way I tried to bury myself under dirt once. I unlock the door and dash up the stairs.

"Jessie?" Mother calls from the kitchen. "That you?"

"Yes," I call down. "I'm taking a nap."

There is silence as I creep the rest of the way. I stop in the bathroom and take a long drink from the faucet before climbing under my blankets and slipping into another consciousness.

* * *

44

"Jessie," someone says, way too soon. "Dinnertime. Wake up."

I open my eyes to darkness and smell Keith's after-practice stink in my room.

"In a minute," I say, wanting to fall back asleep but I know tonight we'll sit down at the big table and have a real family dinner. I get up and even manage to fix my hair and wash my face before I go downstairs, an effort that seems as difficult as if I were doing it underwater.

The dining room, which usually doubles as a workspace for Mother and home to her incessant realty paperwork, is candlelit. The table is silvered and crystalled, shining sweetly against the dark wood of the walls. I see Dad seated at the head of the table, forking potatoes onto his plate and smiling at Mother. Even Keith has cleaned up and has his freshly-showered wet hair slicked back. It's rare to see Keith clean these days. I look at them all, at Mother handing Keith the platter of brisket, and I wonder when the last time it was that I talked to them, like real people, like family. There's always the usual pass-the-butter and school-was-fine conversations at these rare family dinners when we're all actually home at once, but I haven't told one of these people how I've really felt in a long time, and I even bullshit Michael half the time when I really "talk" to him. Dad always says I can talk to him anytime but he means about Jimmy's latest game or my school work, not the important stuff. I sigh as I take my seat. I take a long drink of my ice water, the ice cubes clatter to the bottom of my empty glass.

Mother notices the headband pulling back my hair. "You look nice, Jessica." I smile meekly up at her and take the meat platter and put some on my plate. I will sit here and eat this food and I will stuff it down inside of me like the words that will never leave my lips, I think. I will stay full of the words and the meat and I will be silent forever and smile and nod and be polite and no one will be upset.

"So Jimmy's game was a real upset last week, I hear," Dad says, and I stare at him blankly. Did he just ask me why I'm upset? I wonder at his psychic way of drawing me out and I think of The Granddaughter.

"Yes," I admit, and a lump grows in my throat, the food wanting out, the words coming up. *Oh God!*

"He's a good player, he could get a scholarship. I'm sure his dad's counting on that, pass the butter, Keith-O," Dad says, smiling and winking at me.

I blink and think, here we go. I even look behind me to be sure The Granddaughter isn't standing there, everything feels so surreal.

"You want some melted butter for your asparagus, Greg?" Mother asks.

"No thanks, Diane, this will do," Dad replies, and I feel my head pop. I completely freak out.

"Wait . . ." I hear myself say. "Wait. Please don't talk anymore. I have to say something."

The table becomes too quiet, the forks stop scraping the plates, the candlelight seems to intensify as the outside sky dims to violet after the sunset. The chewing stops, the wall clock stops, the breathing stops, the world stops. The lump moves in my throat, the pain building.

"I'm sorry," my mouth says without my permission. The words hang there. Dad doesn't get it.

"Sorry? About what, sweetie?" he asks, and Mother places her hand on his and nods toward me. Dad's lips purse together as if battening down the hatches, expecting a storm. Keith squirms, the only movement besides the flickering candles in the room.

46

"I owe you all an apology. For last year. For trying to kill myself. God, I'm so sorry! I thought you were all . . . I don't know . . . overreacting or something. I even thought it was your problem, not mine. But now I see that the problem is something I made, like a mess I made and didn't clean up. I get it now, that I caused this thing, this broken thing to happen to our family. I don't even know what I broke, trust or something, but now I get it that I totally messed up, and that what I broke can't be fixed. I don't know how to fix it."

I sob. The tears I thought had dried out of me come back. Keith cries too, hiding behind his hands. Dad looks like the storm hit him. Mother stares at me. She stands, comes over to me, lays her cool hands on my head and helicopters behind me, smoothing my hair as she presses my head into her belly.

"Oh, Jess," she says with a cracked voice. "I've waited such a long time to hear you say that to me."

Chapter Nine

In my room the time nears dangerously to two a.m. and my head is fevered as those words echo in my head, Mother saying that she's waited to hear me apologize for so long. I can't figure out why I feel so restless inside. It's like there's something missing, like the time Jimmy said I love you and I didn't say it back. An awkward silence from Mother's end. Maybe she owes me an apology, I think. Maybe I'm not the only one around here with a reason to apologize. She's the one who is never home, never helps me get organized, never helps me with my laundry or checks my homework or goes to Back-To-School night. She's the one with the "backup" job in case dad ends up in between gigs for more than a month or so, which has only happened twice in his whole career. She's the one obsessing over something she calls The Number, which I don't even get but which causes her and Dad to fight sometimes and which has something to do with their future retirement funds. I toss in my bed, too warm, too uncomfortable to be in my skin. I want to strip naked and run outside in the moonlit night and just escape those stupid words in my head . . . I'm sorry. There's no hope for rest; my brain is full of apologetic phrases trying to claw their way out like those feral cats they have to cage sometimes at the studio lots.

I look out my window that faces the front yard and see that weird yellow glow of the city, of the dangerous Hollywood night that is only minutes away if I were a bird and could fly there. The cats in my head are nearly loose and I can't take it any more. I suddenly wish The Granddaughter were here but I don't really know how to find her. Impulsively I pick up my cell phone and call Jimmy. I let it ring once and quickly hang up and shove my phone under the pillow cuz I can't remember if the ringer is turned on or not. When he calls back the dark pillow-cave lights up as my phone rings in a muffled way. I open my cell and whisper hello into the phone.

"It's freakin' two in the morning!" Jimmy complains. "I can't believe you just called me."

"Sorry," I say, embarrassed. I feel like hanging up. "I can't sleep," I say lamely. "I was hoping you would come and get me. I just need to be with someone."

There's a pause, and a quiet groan. "Jesus! It's a school night."

I can picture him in his boxers, with his beautiful strong chest propped up on his pillows while he talks to me.

"I'm not depressed or anything, Jimmy," I say quickly, feeling the pulse of the night quickening in me. "It's weird, I just feel . . . restless."

"Restless! Jess, you're nuts. I've got a chem test tomorrow, and Coach says if I botch it I'm out of the next game. I fell asleep studying tonight at the kitchen table!"

"Well, let's go get some coffee and you can cram till school starts."

"I can't Jess! I'll be too tired to think."

I'm in a reckless mood, and now I really want to go out and play. "I'll make it worth your while, Jimmy. Please?"

There's another pause on his end and I know I got him. He sighs, a little laugh coming out of the end of it like an exclamation mark.

"Fine." I can almost hear him thinking, those wheels spinning in his head. A thrill runs through me. "Meet me in fifteen minutes. I'll pull up so your parents won't hear me," he says.

"The usual spot," I say, meaning in front of old deaf Mr. Finney's house. He's the only neighbor whose name I happen to know because he's the only one who doesn't care or watch to see what I do. When you've brought emergency vehicles to your quiet neighborhood in the past, people watch you out their windows, I've noticed.

I throw on some rumpled jeans and a sweatshirt, stuff three breathstrips in my mouth, and pouf up my hair with my fingertips. Quieter than the cats in my head I slip down the wood-floored hallways, knowing which creaky steps to avoid. Soon I'm by the kitchen door, opening it just enough to get out, and when it's closed, I'm free.

The night is balmy, not cold, not warm, yet I shiver as I wait for my ride. Even though I'm sneaking out and disobeying house rules, I see it as part of my therapy. Jimmy will help me through this chaos, this noise in my head that makes sleep elusive and thoughts haywire. It will all stop after I see him. Soon that patchy red and gray-primered car that he's been working on for over a year zips past and pulls up at Mr. Finney's. I race silently toward the idling convertible. I see not one curtain flutter back as I fly over the stuck passenger door and land safely in the seat. We race off into the night.

We park overlooking the Hollywood Hills in a deep cul-de-sac leading to gated estates. These residents of suburban L.A., that weird stretchy city of lights crisscrossing beside the Pacific, are protected by alarms, guard dogs, and security personnel so they don't care much what happens on the street outside their mansions. We snuggle under the blanket after taking in the view.

"I had an actual conversation with my family," I tell Jimmy and he nods, stroking my thigh through my jeans as he tunes the radio station. "I actually apologized for trying to kill myself last year. Michael will just shit when he hears."

"Michael? Oh yeah, your shrink." Jimmy leans over and kisses me. I kiss him back, glad for the minty breathstrips I used.

"Yeah, my shrink. Mother told me she'd been waiting to hear it, can you believe it? Like she had nothing whatsoever to do with anything."

"Well, she didn't really, you know," Jimmy says, kissing my throat. Shivers go down my spine but his words confuse me.

"What do you mean?"

"She wasn't really there. It isn't about her," Jimmy clarifies. I think about what he means by this and Jimmy moves the hair from the back of my neck and kisses me there, my weakest spot. He turns my face toward him and kisses me again, deeply. His hands are impatient. He gropes me as the city hums beneath us and I respond, my body acting on its own accord, the cats in my head curled up now and purring sweet dreams. His warm hands slip under my clothes and I push Michael's words away, wanting to pretend that I can just do this without any repercussions. His kisses engulf me like flames, and I feel like I'm leaving my body, my head melting into his heat. His infernal mouth and hands dampen me, the wetness and closeness of him overtaking my senses. It's so ethereal, just being completely physical. I'm about to let go, to let it finally happen this time, when Jimmy pulls away for a moment to reach into his back pocket.

"I've got something," he pants, and he's quick to take a condom out, and open the package with his teeth, and suddenly his warming hands are on me again, and we're revving up, and his kisses are on my throat, his hands are unbuttoning my jeans, that sensation that has me surrendering. I arch my back, my head against the passenger door, my hands up under his shirt feeling his back and chest. He unzips his pants but the gearshift is in the way, things get complicated, and suddenly we realize he can't get to me in this position.

"Let's move to the back," Jimmy says, whispering hot breath into my ear as we struggle over the leather seat. Soon we're in that cramped space, me on the bottom, him on top, red and black leather seats like a casket around me, the sky echoing the city lights above the tree line. The sensation of being buried overtakes me, and I'm suddenly frightened. The words of The Granddaughter come to me: Continuing your relationship with Jimmy Becker will stop the line of the human race as it is destined. And I completely wig out.

"Get off!" I yell, hitting Jimmy in the chest, and that seems to spark him because now he's even more excited and pulling down his pants, holding my hands above my head so I can't move.

"I mean it, Jimmy, I'm not playing around! Stop it! I'm not ready!" He crushes me and pins me with the weight of his chest, and manages to pull down my jeans with one hand. His mouth mashes my words back inside of me and I can barely breathe, let alone speak.

Just as I feel him getting ready to end not only my own virginity but the fate of the world, he leaves a small space beside the edge of the seat and I pull my leg up and he spills forward onto the floor of the back seat and I wriggle my way out from under him. I slide up onto the back of the convertible, pulling up my pants quickly and buttoning them. Jimmy unsticks himself and comes up fuming with rage. I'm ready to jump out of the back of the car but he doesn't come after me. He looks really disappointed, disgusted, even.

"My God, Jess, what the hell are you trying to do to me?" he asks as he pulls his pants up, painfully. I feel bad and start to cry.

"I'm sorry," I tell him, and I am. I wish I could just do it, or get this guy out of my head. He's driving me crazy because all I want is to be with him, but I can't.

I tell him, "I want to, Jimmy. You know I do, but I got scared. It felt like you were crushing me."

Jimmy climbs into the driver's seat and I get in on my side. I buckle myself in and touch his arm. He pulls his arm away.

"Don't touch me." He sits for a moment to compose himself before he starts up the car engine. I've seen Jimmy pout before and I know he won't talk to me now.

"I'm sorry," I say again. He backs up and we head toward home in silence. The cats are up again, yowling for release in my brain. They're really pissed off but there's no place to set them free.

Chapter Ten

I'm tired but the only thing that fills my mind is that look Jimmy gave me when he dumped me off at home and drove away. A million bullets couldn't hurt like that. I wish I could erase that look from my brain.

I want to be alone but I hear the humming noise and can see the blue light emerge in the corner of my room. The Granddaughter shimmers in. I bury my head under the pillow.

"Do not hide, Jessica," The Granddaughter says. "Remember, I can feel your pain. Do not be afraid to show me what you are experiencing."

"Go away," I tell her in my sheet-muffled voice.

"You called me," she says. I sit up.

"That was hours ago!" I say, wiping my tears on my sleeve.

"That was moments ago, with your tears. Your tears over Jimmy Becker."

I stare toward her but find I can see her features better if I look slightly away from her. She is like a fountain of blue light, a calming and serene miracle with a sweet smile and delicate high cheeks. She is beautiful, and I soften to her. She is a part of me.

"You must be happy," I tell her.

"Why do you say those words?"

"Because Jimmy Becker dumped me. It's over between us. He's so mad at me!"

"Are you using irony, or sarcasm, when you say I must be happy?" The Granddaughter muses. "Do you think that your relationship with Jimmy Becker is now over?" The Granddaughter's eyes glow a deep gray, and I sense an intensity from her, as if we are nearing a crucial point in her very existence.

"Yes, it's over." But then I think about it. He's hurting and I messed him up, sure, but isn't that just normal relationship angst? I mean, we've been dating for six months, and we can get through stuff. We got through the Cheerleaders From Hell hating me, his parents having conniptions because he was dating me, my own traumas of being Suicide Girl of Hollywood High . . . why can't we get through this? This is private, between only us. With this problem, we don't even have the eyes of the high school world on us. We can work it out. For the first time since Jimmy drove off I feel better. I smile.

"No, it's not over." My head is swimming and I feel faint when she gets into my head this way.

"Perhaps not," says The Granddaughter. "Tomorrow will give you more information, as it is in this world. Yet there is something I came here to discuss with you. You love Jimmy, is that not so? And tonight there was a special closeness between you. Yet you did not go to Jimmy with love, but with fear. Why is that?"

Was she spying on us? How creepy is that?

"I am merely feeling your emotions," The Granddaughter reassures me.

"Why do you say fear?" I ask, exhaustion finally hitting a home run as we rehash my almost- sex life.

"Fear is the emotion that seized you tonight, Jessica."

Hell yes, I think. *Sex is scary.*

"Why do you fear being intimate with the man that you love?" The Granddaughter asks.

I wonder. Is it having sex, or having to live with knowing that I did it, and that if I'm not careful I could become pregnant, or get some freakoid disease, or that Michael would find out and be disappointed, or my parents would freak out, or that Jimmy would finally get what he wants from me and not need me anymore? I want to cross out that last thought but The Granddaughter nods slightly.

"Wait . . . don't think that I'm holding sex over Jimmy's head so he'll stay around! No way! I want to have sex with him! All the time! You don't know how bad . . . but in this world, there are things to think about. Like disease, and babies, and stuff that can make a wretched life even worse."

"You believe your life is wretched? Why is that?"

I hear a pop, like my brain exploding. I feel like I'm with Michael on the verge of one of his "breakthroughs." I can't go on. Shit.

"My life isn't wretched . . . it's just . . ." and damn, here come the tears. Why am I so messed up?

"Why do you think you are 'messed up,' as you call it?" The Granddaughter asks.

I can't tell you how bizarro it is to have someone say . . . in fact, not even say, I don't know anymore if The Granddaughter speaks or telecommunicates or what, but to have someone answer your private thoughts as if you spoke them out loud. It's way sketchy, and I can't take it anymore.

56

"Please just leave! Go! You're making my life too weird! For all I know, you don't exist, and I'm just an effin' nut case!"

"You do not believe that, do you, Jessie? You do not appreciate confrontation from me, I understand. But I ask you again, tell me why your life is 'messed up.'"

She is stubborn, like me. Of course she's my descendant. Of course she's here to torment me and show me how stubborn I am. Damn her!

"Well," I begin, and I feel sad because I realize, when I look at it, there isn't much to say. Sure Dad is never around, but when he is, life is great, and as Michael pointed out, that keeps the sweetness in our family, the fact that we appreciate him so much. It may even be what keeps my parents married. I mean, how could Dad stand Mother's carping if he had to hear it every damn day? And Keith, sure he sucks, but he doesn't really hurt me. Kara's older brother used to beat her up and broke her arm once. Compared to that shit, Keith's an angel. And Mother . . . whatever. She can't be more than she is. I have food, clothes on my back, and even though I've felt twenty-one since I was twelve, doing (or not) my own laundry, cleaning the house, watching Keith until I went on strike . . .

"Hey!" I say out loud, and for a second I forget that she has been listening to the noise in my head all along. "That's the problem. Mother got pissed off when I quit ballet so she made me take care of Keith in eighth grade! I had to take him everywhere on the bus, to all of his lessons and games. Then when I decided I wasn't her personal servant and she had to start hiring college students to drive him around after school, that's when it went bad! She was always mad at me, and Keith got uptight about it too --" The whole thing fits together like a puzzle piece, and a flood of understanding comes to me. A missing link. My life sucks because I stood up to my mother. My sobs surprise me.

"You are your own person within your family, even if they resent you for it," The Granddaughter says. "Are you your own person with Jimmy Becker as well?"

The question hangs there, not waiting for an answer. She shimmers away as Dad opens the door.

"You okay, Princess? I got up to get some water and I heard talking."

I'm a wreck in my sleeping sweats and T-shirt, my hair is a disaster, my face a flood of tears. I sit in the yellow glow of the hall light. I wipe my face and Dad sits beside me on my bed. He holds me close to him, into his chest. I sob more, the words drained from me, but at least he doesn't ask me what's wrong.

We're late for school, as usual, and since I already had an emofest with Jimmy, my dad, and The Granddaughter last night, I only let myself think about Kara. She called me as I was getting ready for school and I couldn't talk long but she wants to meet for lunch. I'm thinking of ditching fifth period so we can have more time to talk, but I don't know what to tell her that will make me still appear sane.

When we get out of the car at school, Keith and his twerp friends run off, trying to make it to class before the second bell. I saunter onto campus. My teachers all know my mother is a flake and they don't like to confront me without backup anyway. I notice a gathering of cheerleaders and football players by the flagpole, and they are all staring right at me. Not in a kind way either.

"You hole!" Cristabelle Jenners yells at me, and I'm speechless. I have no idea what's happening. My bleary eyes scan the crowd for Jimmy, but he's not there.

"You Goddamned bitch!" says Zane Peck, the halfback. "Thanks to you we lost our best player."

Their glares are murderous, and I rush by trying not to get too near, but it's too late. Molly Johnston is on me. Her long cheerleader leg glides out from under her miniskirt and I trip over her foot. I land on my elbows and feel the burn of grit and blood. My chin hits the asphalt and flesh splits open. I gather myself up, determined not to cry in front of them as I hold my chin. My ankle gives out as I try to stand up and the fullback, Brent Ray, bends down, pretending to help me pick up my backpack.

"I talked to Jimmy, I know what you did. If we were alone right now I'd give it to you, you whore," he whispers, shoving my backpack into my arms. I straighten up and limp bleeding to the nurse's office.

In the health office I'm shaking as Nurse Hayden dabs hydrogen peroxide on my elbow with a clean white pad. My chin has a butterfly bandage on it and I'm too scared by Brent's words to cry or say a word.

"So you tripped?" Nurse Hayden asks, gazing at me suspiciously. I nod. She writes in her accident report.

"We'd better ice and wrap that ankle, it's swelling up." I nod again, folding my arms over my chest. The principal sticks his head in the door. Nurse Hayden is wrapping a flat ice pack around my ankle and fluffing the polyester pillows. Mr. Hicks asks her to leave; she scurries out.

"Hello, Jessica," Mr. Hicks says, sitting on the tissue-covered hospital bed across from me. There is a crinkling noise.

"Hello," I reply in the quietest mouse voice.

"I heard what happened." I expect that he might be here because he knows about this injustice that happened to me and he wants to get to the bottom of it, but I don't want to talk about it. It doesn't matter anyway, because I have it all wrong.

"It was an accident," I say. He stares at me in a strange way.

"I don't know how you can call sneaking out at three a.m. and having sex with our star athlete an accident, Jessica. That's an interesting choice of words. That seems like it must have taken a lot of thought and planning, quite frankly."

My teeth clench tight. I don't know what to say, how to defend myself against a half-truth. I open my mouth but words elude me.

"Mr. Becker called me at five a.m., Jessica. At home. Alex Becker and I go way back, but it's not fun taking a call about your students at that time of day. He caught Jimmy sneaking back into their house. Alex told me Jimmy said that you called him around three a.m. to go out and have sex with him, and that he didn't want to . . . did you know he had a chemistry test today, Jessica?"

I nod dumbly.

"Well, he won't get to take it because he's suspended. Alex asked me to suspend him to teach him a lesson about responsibility. I considered not doing it because he's already on academic probation from the football team, but Alex insisted so Jimmy's off the team. I think it's harsh." Mr. Hicks leans in and gets in my face as my mind scrambles in disbelief.

"But he didn't act alone, Jessie. You're his accomplice, and you have been on probation since we let you come back to this school this year. You know our recommendation for

60

you was the continuation high school. So I'm going to suspend you as well, and maybe next time you'll think twice about your actions and how they affect other people. Jimmy Becker was never a great student but he is a great ball player. There are colleges courting him, Jessica, you know that! How could you so selfishly take that all away?"

"I didn't," I say in my mouse voice.

"Excuse me?"

"I didn't. I didn't have sex with Jimmy Becker. I'm a virgin."

Mr. Hicks stares at me like I'm nuts. "Are you denying sneaking out with Jimmy Becker last night, calling him, asking him to see you?"

I consider denying it to save myself, but if I do Jimmy won't ever talk to me again. I shake my head.

"Very well, Miss Allen. I'll be calling your parents to come pick you up. You're dismissed from school until next Monday. You'll have to make up your schoolwork after that time so you don't fail your courses, if your teachers are willing to make an arrangement with you."

Mr. Hicks leaves the sick room. I sit in stunned silence, trying to decipher what just happened. Nurse Hayden comes back in and checks on my ankle, her eyes avoiding mine.

Chapter Eleven

In the high school main office a bustle of students, intercom calls, and secretaries on phones makes it easy for me to disappear on the uncomfortable wooden bench. Luckily a fight broke out in a classroom so two boys being held apart like mad dogs are brought in, so I don't have to sit in the principal's office. I have loaner crutches leaning against my knee, and my elbows are stinging and bandaged with white gauze, my chin is taped up. I slip my cell from my backpack and call Kara.

"Hey, girl," she says. "Still on for lunch today?"

"No," I tell her in a low voice, my hand over my mouthpiece. No one notices me. "I'm sitting in the office at school, about to be sent home. I got suspended."

"Damn!" Kara says, a laugh in her voice. "What the hell did you do now, Jessie Allen?"

In spite of everything, I have to smile. Yet behind the smile hot tears collect in the corners of my eyes. I'm suddenly so grateful for Kara's friendship.

"I snuck out last night to meet Jimmy, and we both got popped."

Kara laughs again. "I hope you at least had some fun first. I can hear the prison gates slamming from here."

"You have no idea. Jimmy got kicked off the team and we're both suspended, and the Jock Squad tried to kill me when I got here this morning." Though my voice is quiet, the words feel heavy as I say them.

"Shit, Jess! You've always hated those jocks . . . now you can thank them. They'll finish the job for you."

I'm reeling as her words sink in. What is she saying? Is that how she sees me, too? As someone who doesn't want to live? I thought she understood me better than that.

"It's not funny," I say quietly, turning in my seat to face the wall as the tears run free and warm down my face. "Everyone's really mad at me. I don't know what to do."

"I'm sorry Jess," Kara says quickly. "I didn't know it was that serious. You know about stupid suicide humor! I'm such a loser."

"Kara, don't . . ." I say, wiping my eyes. "It's okay. It's just . . . I made this breakthrough with my parents yesterday! I thought things were going well, and now, my mother is going to lose it. I don't even know how my dad will take it. I completely screwed everything up!" My voice grows louder.

The room goes quiet, the talking on phones stops. I look up and everyone in the office is staring at me. I glare back and they look away, going back to their business.

"Can you wait a sec?" I ask Kara.

"Hell, yes. I'm standing in the hallway at school in front of my English class. They're just in there reading novels or some crap to waste time until lunch."

I clip my cell phone onto my shorts waistband, put in the earpiece and pick up the crutches, and limp to the cement planter outside the main office to sit on the wide-tiled lip. A sweet cool breeze refreshes me. I'm alone.

"I'm back. I don't know, Kara . . . I'm tired. Not just from being out late, but from living. Living is exhausting me. Is it supposed to be so hard? What about all that life we see on TV, where people are happy and funny and they get into madcap adventures and everyone leaves smiling and hugging at the end? Doesn't that world exist for anyone? Is everyone as miserable as I am?"

"I am," Kara says in a soft voice. "For one. But don't ask me. I'm not a good judge of reality, Jess. I go to school with a pregnant fourteen year old who was raped by her brother's friend, a seventeen year old mother, a kid who watched his parents get gunned down, and another suicide kid. These are my peers, Jessie, all the rejects in the entire school district. I have no clue what you're talking about, with the hugging and the funny. That's so not my world."

"It's not my world either, Kara. I just don't get it. It's like we all drew a card at birth, that says either 'Fairy Tale Ahead: Live Happily Ever After' or the one I got, which reads 'Everything Sucks: Give Up Now.' How come we didn't get that other card? It's so flippin' unfair."

"I know," Kara says. "But you know what Marsha says: 'You deal with the hand you're dealt'. I mean, for a shrink, she's not always an ogre. She tries to make me deal with the reality I'm in, even if it sucks the majority of the time."

"I guess, for a shrink, Michael's not an ogre either. My mother . . . that's a whole other story." I have this weird urge to tell Kara about The Granddaughter. "And I have a new shrink of sorts, one I haven't told you about yet. She says . . ."

There's a disturbance on the other end, and Kara whispers, "Gotta go, Jess! They sent the National Guard out looking for me. I'll call you later!"

I wonder if I'll still have a cell phone when she calls or if it will be taken away along with every other privilege I have. I say goodbye but she's already gone. I hang up and think of texting Jimmy but see my parents walking up the stairs toward the office. Mother's lips are tightly pursed; Dad looks defeated. I sigh and gather up my belongings and pull myself up on my crutches, glad to have them. The sight of my parents makes me feel weak in the knees.

Chapter Twelve

Downstairs I hear Mother on the phone with Michael's office.

"No way to see him now? I see. Can we at least make an earlier . . . I mean, a longer appointment? She's in crisis, I'm telling you. Yes. Please call me back as quickly as you can."

My bedroom door is open and I sit on the bed, my ankle propped on a pillow. Dad gave me some aspirin and then did that foot-propping thing for me while Mother frantically starting calling my shrink. *Crisis.* I want to call Jimmy but I remember Brent Ray's words. Not the part about him giving "it" to me --what an asshole! But about the lie he told me that Jimmy talked to him. Jimmy would never have called Brent to dis on me! No way! But then how the hell did everyone on campus already know what happened before I even got to school? And why the hell am I suspended? I didn't even get into trouble at school. That is completely unfair, and as soon as Dad comes back up here, I'm going to tell him to fight my suspension. I sit and fume, trying to come up with a way to get Dad on my side.

The Granddaughter appears beside me and I wish I could hop up and shut the door for privacy (in case my parents can see her too) but I don't want to use the crutches or undo the pillow propping. The Granddaughter turns and faces the door and it closes silently shut in an unhurried way.

"You are experiencing pain," she says to me. I nod, still amazed by the whole door closing thing. "Are you agreeable to my easing your discomfort?" I nod again, not really sure what she means. She places her hands, which each have a thumb-like appendage and three long fingers, over my ankle. It warms up. Then she does the same on my elbows and my cut chin. Afterwards I feel all tingly inside but the pain is gone. I put my ankle on the floor. I put weight on it. I stand up and nothing . . . no pain. I flop back on the bed and grin up at The Granddaughter.

"That's so cool! How did you do that?" I ask, peeling off the bloody butterfly bandage on my chin and shaking it free of my fingertips on the nightstand.

"Many can heal with their hands here on Earth, even during your lifespace." I translate lifespace as lifetime, since The Granddaughter has that whole time aversion thing going on.

"According to the legends of the ancient text known in your lifespace as The Bible, Jesus Christ was but one of the great hands-on healers of this planet. You could do it also, Jessica, with the proper training."

"Me? No, not me," I say, feeling uncomfortable with her comparing me on any level with Jesus Christ in the same sentence. I'm not really religious . . . I went to church as a kid, but when Dad was gone a lot and Mother started working, we quit going because our Sundays were too busy getting ready for what Mother called The Habi-Trail . . . the school, dance, and work week, where we were scheduled down to the last second but really we were just going around and around this big tube thingy called life and we always ended up right back where we started, frantic on Mondays.

"What is this thing, this . . . Habi-Trail?" The Granddaughter asks me, and I forget she reads my mind. "I am for some reason picturing small rodents crawling through modular devices."

I suppress a giggle. "A Habi-Trail is a home for hamsters, little fat tail-less mice thingies some people keep as pets, er, animal companions. But I say it because it means the rat race, you know, always running around, being on a schedule, never really getting anywhere."

"And with no real meaning or purpose," The Granddaughter concludes. I nod, not sure if she's right. I mean, if there's no purpose, what the hell are we all doing? Isn't there somehow meaning or purpose in going to the grocery store, to getting us to school and going to work, to getting the car washed and picking up the dry cleaning, those things Mother has on her calendar every single week? I try and glean what the meaning is but I am lost to identify it. Are we really so mindless?

"The people of Earth are farmers," says The Granddaughter, and for a moment I have no clue what she means. "Now. In my Time, as we say between us. The farmers care for Earth. They grow their own foods, nourish themselves with what the planet has to offer them. They are gentle upon the earth and they use its many resources wisely."

"You're a farmer?" I ask, stunned. Somehow I can't picture The Granddaughter getting dirty. She's more of a sit-down inside kind of girl. I forget she knows I think this until I see her mouth move into that familiar triangle.

"I am not a farmer, but of those who are, they sustain themselves in the Habi-Trail by following the daily course of what Earth provides, much in the way your ancestors did."

"Wait a sec . . . you're saying that all the people on earth during your lifetime are farmers? What about lawyers? Movie stars? Computer geeks? Businessmen? What happened to them? "

The Granddaughter nods. "These are vocations of your lifespace only, Jessica. And of course your immediate descendants of the next hundreds of generations. But not of what you call the future, of my lifespace. And the reason for that is you."

I feel faint like I might pass out. "Me?" How is it possible that I caused the end of all careers? Now I can feel it, like a leech in my head sucking out my sanity . . . I am crazy. Certifiable. And The Granddaughter is definitely my hallucination. Pretty soon I'm gonna go downstairs and paint a sign that says 'The End Is Near' and start parading down Hollywood Boulevard.

"You are not suffering mental incapacitation, Jessica. I must assure you, I am astrally here. And this truth I am about to tell you will make you understand why. You are the link to a future, Jessie. A future that saves the fate of the planet Earth."

My mind quiets down and I just listen. I feel as if she is somehow opening my mind up a little wider so I can hear her words.

"The humans cohabitating on the planet Earth in the space of my living are called Guardians, Jessie. They are chosen ones, the ones descended from the old people, your people. They are the farmers. There are not many of them compared to your population in this time of your lifespace."

"If you aren't one of them, these human chosen ones or whatever, then who are you?" I ask, my voice disintegrating into a mere whisper. Suddenly I fear The Granddaughter. I feel I was right all along to think she was an alien.

"Let us use that analogy, Jessie, since it so pervades your mind. In the fact that I am not from this planet at this time and that I come from another dimension, then yes, I am an alien. To you and your kind, I would be what you call an extra-terrestrial. Not of this Earth. But my kind are human, direct descendants of you. My ancestors are The Guardians. We are a race born of the planet Earth once, generations ago to me, in the future to you. You have the bloodline, the beginning of the future race of humans that will ultimately find a way to heal the damaged planet called Earth, within you. I am of Guardian descent. The Guardians are my people. You and one other living in your lifespace have my bloodline. And the other is not Jimmy Becker."

"If not Jimmy, who? What other person, guy, could possibly want to get tangled up with me? Look at me! I'm a mess! I'm barely here myself and now the fate of the world rests on my head, I get it! But I don't want to believe it! If you're here, then doesn't that mean if what you say is true, that no matter what I do, I will generate this future race?"

"There are many realities, Jessie. In your 'time', and as I have made clear to you, we do not use that term in my realm, you humans view time as a linear, direct, and limiting thing. We have come to understand time as an ongoing, simultaneous entity. The only thing that exists is today, right now, this moment. All else is but a memory, a fragment, something that you can perhaps remember,

70

discuss, maybe laugh or cry about but it is not Now. It does not exist. Time is the place that your being is experiencing at that moment. And once that is understood, time can be moved. Time is wherever you wish your 'now' to be."

I have to close my eyes for a moment and I feel a strange stretching sensation on my head, as if The Granddaughter is trying to open my mind even further. I try to resist it but suddenly the information she is giving me congeals and I begin to understand.

"So if time is like a place, not just a concept, then I could come with you to the future . . . what I call the future?" I say, dazzled. In the aura of her blue light my room has disappeared all around me, my bed has become a cloud, and I feel as if I am halfway there with her already.

"You could, but that is not your purpose and not your destiny. I am here because of your blood, because of who you are. It is your blood co-mingled with another's that starts the beginning of an enlightened era, one in which humans begin to see the Earth."

"What does that mean, see the Earth? Travel?" I ask, my bed-cloud lifting me higher.

"Not travel. See, experience, the Earth. Understand the Earth as a living, dynamic planet. Understand the Earth as a being. Hear her shouts of warning, feel her pain."

"I get it," I say. *Excellent.* My great-great-great whatever is a friggin' tree-hugging hippie. I try to hold on to stay on her level but I'm feeling disappointed.

"It is not what you are thinking. The blood bond you forge brings forth a human of great importance, one who teaches others to see the way she does. She is not recognized for it in her lifetime but she is a messiah, a second coming, as your people would call it."

71

"Jesus? Is a girl?" Crazy world, here I come. Take me away.

"A savior of the earth, perhaps as Christians view Jesus. She is the one who bends the consciousness. Ever so slightly. And through her, and many who come behind her, we become a race of One. The chosen ones, The Guardians, are of the One Race but remain on the planet Earth, and those who do stay keep much the same appearance as you, and do not change significantly in a physical way. My direct relatives have different features than The Guardians of Earth because many millennia ago we left the planet Earth. Those who left here found our features changed to adapt to our new home, in space."

"You left . . . Earth? But you said you were human!"

"We are human. But not Earthlings. We are in space, in crafts of our own design, and that is where we live. When we left we entrusted the earth's well-being with The Guardians."

"But . . . why? Why did you leave?" I can't even imagine it, leaving Earth. I don't even get astronauts. What's up with going to the freezing dark moon when you can stay right here in the warm sun?

"We left to save the planet. The planet was dying. The earth's axis was tilted from too much weight. The population had expanded beyond the earth's ability to provide for so many humans. Water was scarce and had to be artificially made. Nuclear waste from your millennia had blighted entire sections of the planet, rendering those places uninhabitable. If we had not left the planet, the entire human race, and all life on Earth, would have become extinct."

"And I . . . I am the answer to that problem? By breaking up with Jimmy Becker and going on with my life and

72

meeting this person who I will have a child with some day? That's the solution?"

"It is," The Granddaughter says. "It is simply that. It is but one scenario."

"What does that mean?"

"I have projected myself into many of your lifespaces, and I have seen all of the scenarios as they pertain to you. In most scenarios, the human lifeform becomes extinct and the planet Earth dies. That is the outcome the majority of the time."

"Why is that?"

"In one scenario, you did not exist. You were dead. You had succeeded in taking your own life. In another scenario, you had the child of Jimmy Becker at a young age. The relationship did not last. You killed yourself in this scenario as well, this time at a later age. You had no other child. These two scenarios played themselves out over and over again. Until we found the bloodline and were able to trace it back to you. Then we knew we had another option that would save us . . . that you could live."

"I . . . I want to live."

"Of course you do. And you will," The Granddaughter says, shimmering away as the door opens. Mother and Daddy come in, their faces a dark cloud of pent up feelings with loud words about to unleash.

Chapter Thirteen

It is surreal, the way my parents come into my room slo-
mo like bad guys in an action film. I suspect everything
seems to be working in a different time warp because The
Granddaughter did something to my head, something
strange when she poured that information into my brain so I
could understand what she was saying to me about the
future. I stand there by my bed and try to shake the feeling
that I'm just acting out a part, that nothing is real in this
drama. I think it's bizarre that my parents will say their
lines, then I will say mine, and I don't even know what my
lines are now. It dawns on me that it is because my lines are
not now, in the present. They are in the future, in a minute

from now, and The Granddaughter reminded me that only this very second matters, and nothing else does. Finally that thought settles down in my head as the parents stop about three feet away from me, arms crossed.

"Hey," Dad says, pointing to my ankle. "What happened? You look all healed."

"Oh, it still hurts," I say, sitting down on the bed, pretending to be in pain. "I was just testing it."

"But your scratches," Dad points to my chin and my elbows. "They're gone."

"Dad! I covered them up. It's make-up. You of all people should know that. Those cuts and scratches depressed me. "

Dad sits meekly on the end of the bed and nods knowingly--duh, he works in the movie industry--and Mother pulls up a chair from my desk and gets right to the point.

"This needs to stop," Mother says, her voice a frown. Dad looks at me pleadingly. My line comes to me naturally, and I get the weirdest feeling we've all been here before.

"I know, and I agree," I say my line, but this time I mean it. No bullshit. Somehow all those lines back and forth with Michael were like the scripts acted out in movies, the dialog we used to play off each other, and that's what I expected again, but these lines are different. They are coming from the heart, from my true self. Somehow I feel as if my heart was opened a mile wide by The Granddaughter's visit only moments ago. Everything seems so clear.

"I mean it," Mother admonishes, obviously not ready for the new and improved me. "This sneaking out at night, and did you do it, then, Jessica? Did you sleep with that boy Jimmy Becker? After all the things Michael told you about, warned you could happen? You did it anyway?"

Dad fidgets and I can feel him shrinking away, wishing he were someplace else. No wonder he likes to stay away at work so much. He's really like some fish out of water here at home. Mother rules the roost and he's her yes-man. Now I get it.

"I didn't sleep with Jimmy Becker, Mother. I have wanted to, if you must know, for a long time, but I haven't. Virginity intact, even if you are hearing otherwise from questionable sources." Somehow the stilted language of The Granddaughter starts to come out of my mouth. It's unusual but I like it. I see now how she feels . . . so different, so alien even, from the rest of us fellow travelers who aren't even on her plane, can't even understand her very being. I'm more like her than I realized before. She is, in every sense of the words, my kindred spirit.

"Well. . ." Mother's mouth is practically twitching. "You did sneak out though. . ."

"I had many deep thoughts pressing on my mind, Mother. Jimmy is someone whom I have considered an ally during this strange and terrifying time in my life. I see that I was wrong after what has happened today. He obviously cannot be trusted."

Mother is truly dumbfounded and I would be amused except that I feel as if I am on the outside looking in, just watching her struggle internally with the war she thought she was waging versus the one she is actually in. I look at her in a kind and calm way as she pulls together her thoughts.

"This . . . this isn't over, this conversation. And you have an early appointment in one hour with Michael, because I called his office and explained that you were in a crisis and they were able to squeeze you in. But for now I'm too angry to deal with you. I don't care what excuses you have, but

I'm done with this crap, you hear me? I'm done!" Mother gets up and storms out of the room. Dad looks after her as if trying to decide where to be.

"You shouldn't taunt your mother, Jess," Dad says in a sad voice.

"I didn't," I reply, looking into his eyes. "I promise. I've just . . . seen the light, in a way, Dad. And things will change here for the better, I can promise you that."

Dad seems to want to peer inside my head to see if I'm messing with him. I'm not. But he can't tell so he shrugs and pats me on my knee, carefully since he can't tell where my injuries are since he thinks I covered them up with make-up.

"I hope you're right, Jess," he says in a quiet voice. "We need things to get better. This . . . this crappy version of life we're all experiencing, it sucks."

I smile at Dad, that ex-surfer who moved "inland" a few miles to Hollywood to please Mother and joined in the land of make-believe to butter the household bread. There's so much I want to say to Dad all of a sudden, but could he get me now?

"Maybe this isn't the crappy version of our lives, Dad. Maybe this is the one that works out. Maybe the crappy version was the version when you didn't get home in time to find me and I really did die on the bathroom floor, covered in my own blood, alone and confused and desperate. Maybe that's the crappy version and this is the version of our lives that we fix."

Dad can't handle me, and I've gone too far. He stands up and leans on the wall for support, his mouth a tight line, his eyes narrowed in pain and unspent emotion.

"How do you do that?" he asks, his line-mouth now a twisted rope. "How can you just say things like that, just rip a person open by saying things like that and just leave

77

everything lying there? How can you? I don't want to hear that, I don't want to think about that day. . ." Dad cries. I've never seen him cry before. I've never seen him show any negative emotion before. He slips down the wall onto the floor and I can feel that this pain has been wedged in his gut, unyielding, for a long time. The tears come out of him and I feel terrible for him yet I feel him clear the way to hear my words, which are me, but not me.

"I am not trying to hurt you, Dad. I am trying to show you the hope. We are done with that day. It is no longer a part of us. We are here now, we are now on this day. There is no blood here, no pain like there was then. There is still misunderstanding, doubt, shutting down, and also there are even good intentions but that other version of our lives is no longer a threat to us. I will live. I am here now. We can move on."

Dad looks up at me and dries his eyes on the bottom of his Crab Shack T-shirt. I squat down beside him and smile. He opens a door inside of himself and lets me back in his heart. He smiles at me and lets me help him up onto the bed.

"When you were a baby, Jess, I knew you were special," he says, still playing with the bottom of his now-damp shirt. "I wasn't really ready for a kid but when you got here, I was ready for you. And I knew I would always take care of you, always protect you, and I tried. I really did try."

"I know," I say, noticing now how the morning sun fills my walls with clear light that is different, less golden orange and more pale yellow, than the light I've often seen in the evening. I've never really been in my room much this time of day, at ten in the morning. Everything feels so clear in the morning.

"You didn't let me protect you, Jess. That's hard for me to get over."

"But it was you who protected me, Dad. You found me. You saved me. You saved me from something neither one of us expected from me."

"Why did you do it, Jess? What in your life is so wrong that you thought you had no way out, that you had to leave us and everything behind?"

The light is also filled with shadow, I notice. Shadow is a tricky thing. It is an outline of a thing, but not a thing. Right now the shadows are of palm trees outside my windows. They are waving back and forth trying to get my attention. I turn to face my father, this man who is the person I love most in the world yet also, the person who is most like a stranger to me. The light and the shadow. He is both of those things to me.

"Dad, I wish I had an answer," I say, feeling like myself again after channeling that wonky relative of mine from the future, "but sitting here with you now, the only thing I can say is I have no effing idea what I was thinking when I tried to kill myself last spring."

Chapter Fourteen

I'm strung out as I shower, my insides still shaking from my encounter with Dad. I feel so different, and yet as I towel dry my hair I'm beginning to wonder. What the hell is going on with me? What did The Granddaughter do to me when she did that mind probe? Maybe she's not really my great-great whatever from the future and I'm just a teenage alien abductee, someone who is visited by aliens and being prodded, a human lab rat for testing by a foreign species. I pull on my pants to get ready for my shrink appointment. Maybe Michael can help me.

As I put on my lip gloss I want to call Jimmy but there's little time until we have to leave and I'm sure his dad is right there with his cell by his side waiting for me to do just that. It's really starting to bug me . . . how did everyone at school know about what happened between us if Jimmy didn't call and blab to his moronic friends? And if he did call and blab . . . what an asshole. I know he was mad at me when he dropped me off this morning, but seriously . . .

"Jessica? In the car in five minutes. I have to run next door for a moment," Mother calls from below. Five minutes! I can check it out in five.

"Be right there," I reply, reaching for my cell. I speed dial Jimmy and I'm surprised when he answers.

"Jimmy! My God, are you okay?" I ask, caught off guard.

"As well as I can be, seeing as how my life is destroyed," Jimmy says in the crabbiest voice. I hate it when he sulks, but I guess he has good reason.

"Your dad really fell apart, huh? I'm so sorry you got caught sneaking back in! Are you sure the coach won't let you back on the team when your suspension is over?"

"What do you want?" His voice is so mean, so sour. I can tell his dad has been poisoning him against me. It's happened before.

"I just want to make sure you're okay. I'm suspended too, you know. And the rah-rah squad got me when I went on campus today."

"What do you mean?"

"That bitch Molly tripped me, totally messed me up. . ." I'm about to describe my injuries when I remember that The Granddaughter healed me and that I have no marks to prove my case. "Anyway, it was a rough morning. It's so unfair that we're both suspended for something we didn't even do at school! We should report Principal Hicks to the school board for this."

Jimmy is silent, the way he gets when he's gathering his thoughts. I can picture his long black eyelashes resting as his eyes close in concentration. I hear him breathe in like he does after making a decision. I can see his black wavy hair toppling forward over his eyebrows, and yet I'm caught off-guard when his words come.

"We're done, Jessie. I can't see you anymore."

"Look, Jimmy. . ." I stammer. "We're the victims here, can't you see that? We're the ones who were wronged! And if we break up, then everybody else wins! Don't you get it?"

"It's over."

"Is your dad standing right there, making you say that, Jimmy?" I hear a weird sound, like a snicker, but it's coming from Jimmy.

"No, my dad didn't tell me to break up with you. He didn't have to. Last year, before I met you, I knew what I wanted, and I was focused and training to be the best ball player. You were like . . . my screw up, just a mistake. I'm done messing up my life because of you. We're over."

I can't believe what I'm hearing. I can't believe that his dad isn't standing right next to him with a match and a can of gasoline getting ready to torch his beloved car if he doesn't say these horrible words to me.

"That's pretty harsh," I say in a choked voice.

"I know, and I'm sorry. But don't do anything stupid, Jess. I'm not worth it."

I know what he means, he's telling me not to kill myself. It pisses me off that he thinks I'm so fragile.

"I know you're not worth it," I sneer, and I feel better.

"Then I guess we're clear." There's a pause, a pause that means we should hang up the phone. But I'm not done yet.

"Did you tell your friends what happened? Is that how they found out?"

There's another pause that answers my question. I feel something snap inside of me.

"Ah, I told Brent I got caught sneaking out with you. That was it."

And that makes sense, why they all assumed that we had sex last night. Because Jimmy never told any of those friends of his that we have never had sex. They think he's been shagging me all along, and that's why we were together.

"Okay," I say.

"Breaking up on the phone sucks. But it will be a while till I see anyone, since I'm suspended and all. Sorry to hurt you, Jess. Please stay safe."

"I get it. Bye Jimmy."

I hang up and sit on the bed in shock, startled by the impatiently honking horn of Mother's minivan in the driveway.

Lucky for me Mother isn't speaking to me so I am allowed to sit quietly in the front seat and process my thoughts on the way to Michael's office. I feel as if I should be devastated but I have no tears for Jimmy. It's weird, as if something broke inside of me. Not in half, like a broken heart, but something broke free . . . some mysterious invisible cord that connected us once is now detached and we're both just ourselves again. I want to be sad. I think of his eyelashes, of the "J&J" we scratched into the tree by the football field, of the smell of his neck. I feel a longing for him physically but not a sadness of never being with him again. I wonder if my heart isn't a small black charcoal thing incapable of love anymore.

Mother is a stony stare and a stiff lip. She drives too fast and corners too wide, trying to make a point. I want to say something to her but I feel the wall inside of her. Anything I say will end up an argument but I feel a need to slow down her thoughts and her driving.

"Jimmy broke up with me," I offer.

Mother looks surprised, and then her eyes narrow. "I'm not surprised. The one good thing that's happened to you in the last year."

She has no idea he's really the only good thing that's happened to me since I became the social outcast, but I don't say that to her.

"He wasn't so good. He just wanted to get in my pants," I say instead. Mother flies around the corner, her travel mug shooting out of the cup holder and soaring across the width of the van. Wrong tack. We land precariously in both lanes and Mother hits the gas pedal.

"I'm not upset," I say in a soothing voice. "I've figured out some stuff." Mother's foot eases up and the van slows, but we're still speeding. "I need to focus on myself for awhile. Jimmy was like a buffer to my figuring out what happened last year. He took all of my attention, which isn't a bad thing cuz I needed him then, except that I haven't learned how to just be me by myself. That's what I want to work on next. I'll tell Michael today."

"What are you saying?" Mother says, driving the speed limit.

"I don't know. . . I just feel okay to just be myself now. That's all."

Mother is silent, her expression still sharp, but the line of her mouth has softened.

"I'll be here when you're ready to come home," Mother says as she drops me off in front of Michael's office. It's the nicest thing she's said to me all day.

Mother, in her hurry to be rid of me, has dropped me off twenty minutes early for the specially-scheduled appointment. The receptionist, the young one whose name

84

is either Christine, Kristen, or Kirsten, and her nervous checking of the clock, means another client is due for the doctor who shares space with Michael, and she needs me to be out of the way since there's a rule that two clients can't be in the waiting room at once. There might be an uprising.

"Do you mind waiting in Dr. Gelman's office?" she asks quickly.

I shake my head and let myself in. I am alone in Michael's office for the first time. I touch the deep wood of Michael's desk, and pick up a letter opener from the leather pencil holder. It's wood with a rounded point. If I tried to slit my wrists, it wouldn't even scratch me. The only thing it could hurt is one of Buffy's vampires. Intrigued I search for any sharp or dangerous object, just out of curiosity. The lamps cords are cut short and special plugs have been mounted just inches from the lamp base. There are locked safety covers on the plugs. The table and desk have rounded edges. The glass windows are six feet off the ground at their lowest point and . . . yep, safety glass, with wire mesh inside. I wonder if Michael had to buy all these things at a special store, Shrinks R' Us. There is only soft leather and thick rugs and curved knickknacks. This room has been baby-proofed to the nth degree. Somehow I'm disgusted by that.

I sit in Michael's chair, wondering what it is to be such a man who has to watch out for the safety of his fragile-minded patients. His chair is very tall. He's always looking down on me, literally, I think. I never noticed that before. I just thought he was tall. The room I visit twice a week seems strange to me now from this side of the desk. I hear Michael's voice in the reception area and hurry to the other side of room and sit in a different chair than usual, the scratchy floral one, so he'll literally have to see me differently today.

Michael looks harried, probably from having to come into his office early. The man who is normally so neat and organized is a bit breathless and his manila folders are slipping fan-like from under his arm. I feel as if I should help him out but I stay seated. Finally he's sitting at his desk, rearranging his folders, and after a moment he looks up.

"Jessie," he says, as if trying to download the information about me into his brain. It hits me that he is the one always prepared for me. He knows when I'm coming to his office. He has five minutes between clients to sip some water, go over my files, look at his notes about our last conversation and our 'homework', those little life lessons he has me try at home between visits. But the way he stares at me shows me a dark truth: I'm just another client to him. I'm words in a manila folder, I'm the neat blue-penned notes he takes, I'm a stack of papers to be filed and examined at will.

"Are you comfortable?" He seems confused, and I realize it's because I'm sitting in a different spot.

"I'm fine."

"Good. Your mother called me and insists you're in a crisis. Care to tell me what's happening?"

"Well. . ." I say, ready by habit for the bullshit game of lion hunter vs. prey, but it's not in me today. I'm not even careful as my words lope into the open. "I was suspended from school today because I went sneaking out with Jimmy last night and he got caught coming back in this morning."

"You were suspended . . . was he late for school?" Michael is not any less confused by this information. I shake my head.

86

"Exactly my point. It was a bogus charge. Jimmy's dad is an old friend of our principal. He's trying to teach him a lesson in responsibility, so he calls up the principal, Mr. Hicks, who as you know hates me anyway, and gets Jimmy suspended from school and kicked off the football team. I was suspended too as an accomplice. What happened didn't even happen at school! It's completely unfair."

"Football was his chance to get into college, wasn't it?" Michael asks, and I'm glad he didn't have to look something up to know that.

"Yes. That's why it's so unfair. To ruin his son's life to make a point, that's just horrible."

Michael pauses, and I recognize that old hunting-lion look in his eyes. I stumbled into his territory like a willing victim.

"And yet you would be the first to admit that last year you almost ruined your family's lives to make a point," Michael says.

Right for the throat. God, he's good at his job. A week ago a statement like that would have wounded me. I smile a little.

"Good one, you're right."

Michael is right. Sometimes to be a decent human you have to look around and see who might get caught up in your self-inflicted stupidity.

"It's still bogus, though. For Principal Asshole to suspend us both for that just because he's doing his old buddy a favor."

"You should know, Jessie, that there are some things that you have no control over. And here's a life lesson. . . it's not what you know but who you know. It's just the luck of the draw. How did your dad get his job in the movie industry?"

"Well, he had this friend in college . . ."

"Exactly."

Michael's on a roll. This non-game is even more interesting than the old one.

"I get it," I say. Weird, those are the last words I said to Jimmy when we broke up.

"So tell me about your crisis," Michael says. He seems enthusiastic about our new relationship.

"I don't really have one. I should, but I don't. I snuck out because I told my parents yesterday that I was sorry about trying to kill myself last year and we had this big emofest, and then I couldn't sleep and so I called Jimmy and we hung out but he tried to bone me and I wasn't ready so he got mad and took me home and then got caught sneaking into his house and all hell broke loose by the time I got to school this morning."

Michael raises his pen and then lowers it, as if unsure which piece of information is the most important for his notes. He drops his pen onto his desk and folds his hands together. I banter on.

"So I go to school this morning all fa-la-la ready to make up with Jimmy and Molly the bitch trips me, another guy practically threatens to rape me, and then I go to the nurse and the principal sends me home for a week."

"You shouldn't have gone out last night, Jessie," Michael says, and it's the first time he has ever, ever told me I've made an error in judgment. "It was inconsiderate."

"I know. I messed up."

"You're paying for it now."

"Yes. And the last part of it, is that Jimmy broke up with me this morning."

"I see."

Now he does make a note, a long one, in his file on me. I wish I could turn into a fly and buzz over and see what he's writing. I smirk, picturing my thousand fly eyes not being able to read the mega-fractured version of his words.

"You were very close to Jimmy. You counted on him to hold you up emotionally. You must have some strong feelings about your breakup."

"Not really. He told his best friend with the big mouth what happened so everyone at school hates me even more than before, and all along he's been pretending we've been having sex but we haven't so now I think Jimmy's kind of a jerk."

"I see." More notes. I look outside through the high windows and see the palm trees swaying in the warm breeze and realize I have something unusual, a day off, yet here I am in a Beverly Hills psychiatrists' office talking about my breakup and my troubles. This sucks.

"Hey," I say, unexpectedly. "I wanted to ask you something. Do you think I'm crazy?"

Michael stops writing, breathes loudly through his nose, and then shakes his head. "No, not crazy," he says cautiously.

"Depressive?"

He shakes his head again.

"Suicidal?"

No with the head.

"Dangerous to society at large?"

Michael smiles a tiny smile and shakes his head 'no' again.

"Then is it okay if we don't do this anymore? Me coming here I mean. I want to cut back on my therapy. I know it was required for me to get back into school because Principal Asshole has it out for me, but could you write me a note excusing me from twice-a-week therapy so we can both just get on with our lives?"

Michael folds and unfolds his hands on his desk and considers this a moment.

"What would you do to keep your stress managed?"

"Well, I'd like to get a jump on my tan. Just lie in the sun and relax. I haven't done that in a long time."

Michael pauses, his pen tapping the manila folder.

"Use sunscreen," he says, not able to help himself as he licks his lips.

"I will."

"Your mother wants to try antidepressants on you, Jessie, judging by the phone conversation I had with her this morning. But I'm not inclined to agree with her that it would help you. I'm not sure that's a path I would embark on with you, and I was going to let her know today that I feel meds are not a good option for you. She would have probably removed you as my client anyway. I was going to try to prepare you for that."

"Can you just tell her I'm okay? I don't want this anymore. It's just feels so . . . last year."

Michael hides his smile, a bigger one this time, behind the manila folder with my name on it.

"I'll arrange the necessary paperwork with your school if you agree to check in, say, once a month with me about your progress. This is a big step, Jessie. You're going from counting on our visits twice a week to a check-in once a month. Yet we've discussed ways to cope in the real world. This is a good chance to explore some of your options. I'm a phone call away for you in a real crisis."

"Not a mother-made-up-one, I know," I say, standing up. "My mother's downstairs. Want me to get her?"

"Not quite yet. I think that your mother will still be attending my parent support group, as she's quite the advocate in that arena. If she makes the decision to have you come back to me, I want you to promise to comply."

"I will, but things are different now between us. I know she's mad at me but . . . since I apologized . . . it's like this huge boulder was moved out of the way and we can talk again."

"Okay, bring her up and we'll go over our decision with her together. I'll explain to her our options. And remember, this isn't a ten-mile hike, it's a baby step. I'm here if you need me."

"Thanks, Michael," I say, and when he stands up I walk over to him and give him a big hug. It's the first time I've hugged him. He is much shorter than I thought.

Chapter Fifteen

The sunlight in Los Angeles is blinding white hot, like *paparazzi* flash bulbs on the red carpet. We walk outside to the minivan squinting, avoiding the glare of the sun. Once inside the minivan we are safe from the heat.

"Let's get this air conditioner on," Mother says. She backs out of Michael's office parking lot space, and I get a strange pang thinking that I won't be seeing this place again for awhile. It's not a sad feeling, more like one of accomplishment. Like going home from the cuckoo hospital was an accomplishment. We drive toward Santa Monica Boulevard. Mother gets ready to turn left, back toward our house.

"Turn right," I tell her.

"Right? Why?"

"Please?"

Mother shrugs and we head west and soon the traffic becomes snug around us and the ocean pulls us towards Santa Monica's breezes.

"What are we doing here?" Mother wants to know. I can almost hear her protests: You're in trouble, you shouldn't be rewarded for bad behavior, you should be in school . . . there are a million reasons ricocheting around the word 'no' in her brain.

"Can we park?" I ask when we reach the beach. Mother hesitates, but she goes into a nearby garage and we park. We lock the car and walk toward the pier. Mother is digging in her purse for money.

"No," I tell her. I lead her around the pier, onto the beach, and take off my Converse tennis shoes (no socks). I squish my toes in the sand and it feels amazing, like a warming foot massage.

"What about your leg?" Mother asks.

"What?"

"Your injury," Mother says in a quiet voice.

I forgot that just this morning I had been limping, bruised, and sore, until The Granddaughter healed me. It seems like a trillion lifetimes have passed since then.

"I'm fine. Let's go."

Mother follows me across the sand, taking off her own gold ballet flats and walking with her toes pointed, an echo from her own years as a dancer. We spontaneously settle in on the edge of the beach where it slopes to meet the water and watch a few small waves wobble up the shore.

"Michael says you're ready for this."

"I am."

"I hope you're right. I'm scared, Jessica. He's been such a lifeline for me."

This surprises me. I thought Michael was my lifeline, but I guess Mother's right . . . she is the one who calls him when she doesn't understand me, when I'm difficult or "in crisis", as she likes to say. How ironic it is that she uses the word lifeline, as he is the lifeline that saved me after I tried killing myself.

"You'll still go to the support meetings?"

"Yes, but it will seem strange to go when you're no longer in Michael's care."

"You don't have to go."

"I know. We'll see." Mother pushes piles of sand around her feet.

"About last year. . ."

Mother looks at me and shakes her blonde head. It is a simple act but it speaks volumes to me . . . she can't handle that discussion. She is a victim trying to move on, not willing to rehash the night that changed her reality so drastically. *She will never in her lifespace talk with you about your attempt to kill yourself,* The Granddaughter's voice comes into my head. I shade my eyes with my hand and look around but The Granddaughter is not there. Suddenly I understand; Mother's safety zone is the group she attends each week, that's where she goes to cry and anguish over what I've done. She never brings it home. She never will. She's not a cold fish, she's a fierce lioness protecting her household.

I roll up the bottoms of my cargo pants and push my T-shirt up to my bra-line and lie down on the sand. I close my eyes and the warm melon sun caresses me, the waves hum a melody in my ears. I feel Mother adjust herself beside me, her body stretched across the beach next to mine. It feels like the most normal thing on earth to be lying next to her and yet we've been strangers for a couple of years now. I wonder how it's possible that we let time get in our way, Time, a thing that doesn't even really exist, according to my Future Relative. My head swims with a strange heaviness and I want to reach my hand over and hold hers but I

94

instinctively know she can't handle it. Not yet. I keep my hand to myself and we breathe in unison and let our fears leak from our souls and escape into the sand beneath us.

It's dusk when we drive home. Mother is disheveled, her hair unusually windblown and her white button-down shirt has a dirt smear across the front.

"Can we stop at a nursery?" I ask.

"A . . . what?"

"The nursery, you know, where you get your plants."

"Why?"

"I just feel like checking something out."

It's odd, when we walk in, how I remember being dragged here my whole life. With Mother there was always a "quick stop at the garden center" on the way home from ballet lessons, school, the grocery store, whatever. She could run in and load a basket of blooms in about fifteen minutes. She always knew exactly what she wanted.

The smell of soil coupled with a hint of weed killer hits my nose. I lead the way, heading straight to the herbs and vegetables.

"Remember that area by the back fence that you were going to turn into a garden?" I ask.

"That was years ago. I never got around to it."

"Can we do it now?"

"What, make it into a garden? That would be hard. It's all overgrown . . . with bougainvillea, I think, or maybe it's some kind of climbing vine. It would take a lot of work to prepare the soil, especially for vegetables."

"Can we do it anyway? I have some free time right now."

I don't really know why I'm standing here in the garden center with my mother. This has always been her thing, to garden, but something about what The Granddaughter said about the humans left on the earth being gardeners makes me think that there's something to this seemingly boring hobby. I mean, how exciting can it be to watch a bunch of plants grow? But I'm willing to give it a shot if it means I can have something, maybe a stronger connection to what The Granddaughter tells me. Maybe a stronger connection to my mother.

"I guess I can help you tomorrow after work . . ." Mother says, and I hear something in her voice I haven't heard in a long time: Excitement. I smile at her. Another thing that hasn't happened in a long time.

"Okay," I say. We load up our cart with the leafy stems of tomatoes, basil, garlic, squash, and corn as the sun setting over the beach turns the sky pink, illuminating our future garden.

Chapter Sixteen

My hands dig into the earth. This is no easy task because I have been sitting here under these brambles for what seems like a decade. My feet are numb: sound asleep. My arms are torn and bleeding, I have a blister on my palm from cutting away roots with rubber handled pruners, and I'm pretty sure there is more than one spider crawling around in my hair, but finally I am able to push dead moldering leaves aside and discover that brown nirvana I have been seeking, the earth. I feel like rolling around in it, I'm so excited, but it's only a patch the size of both of my dead feet and there's a whole other bush to hack into.

"Jessie," I hear a voice say, and I think it's The Granddaughter. I look around, wondering if I'll be able to see her in broad daylight. I've only ever seen her indoors. I see a shadowy form walking toward me from the house, and I squint to see who or what it is.

"Jessie, it's me!" I hear, and the form moves out of the glaring light into the shade on the back wall of our property. I'm stunned to see Kara standing there.

"Hey!" I yell, wanting to stand up but my tingling feet defy me. I reach up and Kara helps me stand. I stagger, using her arm to balance myself. "What are you doing here?" Kara's never been to my house before.

"Your mom invited me, believe it or not."

I don't really believe it. I have never really talked to my mom about Kara, but I guess she knows all about her through Michael, who introduced us when we both were inpatients last year. Mom may know more about me than I think.

"Well, if I'd known you were coming, I would have put something nice on. . .sorry." I'm suddenly keenly aware of my cut-off overalls with paint splatters on them, my wretched stinky tank top with no bra, and my un-made up face.

"You look how you always do," Kara says, punching me in the arm.

"Watch it!" I say, slugging her back. We laugh, and she points to my impossible pile of brush.

"Some crazy new kind of therapy?" she asks.

"Yeah. Actually it is. It's my own special kind of therapy."

"Good, because I'm here to help."

Kara squats down in the shady undergrowth, her hands illuminated by the sunlight pouring through the trees above. I kneel beside her and massage my feet through my Converse tennies, regaining feeling in my toes. I want to understand it all, how Mom managed to get Kara here, how it all happened, but my words will break the magic of the spell.

"We're building a garden," I say. "From this pile of pain we have to get rid of first. Be careful, it's sharp and thorny."

"Your mom says if we can't handle it she'll have the guy down the street move it out of here," Kara say, eyeing the mass reproachfully. Her black liner outlines her eyes like an Egyptian princess, unused to hard manual labor. I shake my head.

"We have to do it ourselves. It's therapy, remember?" We reach in with pruners and take turns snipping and bagging the thorny stems that threaten to cut open our skin.

"You two are a mess!" Mom says later when she comes down to our secret garden carrying a tray with a lemon-filled pitcher of tea and three tall glasses of ice. She's wearing jeans, a long-sleeved shirt and a bandanna in her hair, and she's armed with flowered gardening gloves in her breast pocket.

"I didn't know I'd be needing to bring the first aid kit! I'd better go grab it," she says as she looks at the gouges on our arms. Kara has a scratch on her nose where a branch bounced back after she cut it, seeking revenge.

"It hurts!" Kara complains, showing her war wounds. "But we're okay for now."

"We're tough," I tell Mom. "We'll be fine."

"I know you are," Mom says quietly. She pulls a small rusted table out from under the big oak tree and brushes the black decaying leaves off the top. She sets the glasses and pitcher down.

"What time is it?" I ask, realizing that Mom is here so something must be up. That evening glow that announces her arrival home from work surely hasn't happened yet.

"It's about two. I took the afternoon off."

99

It's clear now, Kara called for me on our home phone when she couldn't reach my cell, Mom was home early and answered, they talked, Mom invited Kara over. Mystery solved, but the magic of the three of us tackling the shrub from hell hasn't left me. It's sort of been this way all along . . . this is what we've all been through. Mom's been tackling me, the thorny shrub in her life. Kara has her own thorny demons, and lately I've been trying to prune the crazy overgrowth of my own life, though Jimmy Becker was a great way to avoid doing just that. It dawns on me that I haven't really thought of Jimmy since yesterday. I was thinking of the garden all night long, how to get the bed cleared for our new plants. I look at the forlorn vegetable sprigs in the wheelbarrow, waiting for a drink and a transplant, and I dig into the spiny taproot of the second bougainvillea, ready to be rid of it once and for all.

I awake from my Michael-recommended nap and realize that Michael has no say in my life anymore. He doesn't get to know if I'm well rested or not. But I've become hooked on naps and after spending six hours in the garden, I was ready for one. The sunset is nearly over. . . I hear crickets and see the last vestiges of pink in the western sky out my window. Kara left two hours ago with Band-Aids, a sunburn, and a smile, and a promise to return tomorrow for digging and planting day. I know she has to ditch school to help us but I hope she comes anyway and Mom won't figure it out. Mom helped us water the veggies well since we weren't able to get them in the ground. She showed me how to bank dirt and straw around the plant bases in the wheelbarrow, so they wouldn't dry out too much and be susceptible to suffering something Mom calls "transplant shock." I really get the idea of transplant shock . . . it must be wretched to

100

get ripped out of your safe warm little plastic home and dumped in a big pile of dirt in a stranger's yard.

"Shall I heal those for you, Jessie?" A voice comes from nowhere and it makes me jump. This time there is no humming noise or light . . . The Granddaughter is just there. She's shimmering in the corner of my room, pointing at my arms.

"I didn't hear you," I say to her, my heart still racing. The bougainvillea scratches look angry and red even after the heavy dose of first aid cream. Before I can respond I feel a warm tingle and my cuts sort of bubble, turn white and disappear. But I'm actually bummed, like I lost my badge of honor. I can see The Granddaughter giving me a queer look, and I can feel her trying to figure out what I'm feeling. Slowly the scratches, those scabby reminders of my hard day's work, reappear on my arms but they don't hurt anymore.

"Is that satisfactory?" she asks. I know she can feel my approval but I nod.

"How did you do that?" I ask, staring at my arm.

"I relocated space to the moment before I healed your cuts. It was a momentary change in the time/space continuum, as your people call it. I should have waited for your reply. We do not heal without permission."

"But how did you heal it to begin with?" I'm again wondering why she said I could learn to do it last time we spoke. How could I do something like that, like a mini-miracle?

"It is something all humans can do. It is something you can learn to do with your mind. It is the act of picturing yourself whole and healthy, and then applying the healing energy of the universe to the one you wish to heal. I will give you lessons another time, if you like."

The Granddaughter looks distracted suddenly, and her shimmer fades to a dull translucent blue. Suddenly she is her self again, shimmering in that frosty color blue I've become used to. I look down at the scratches on my arms.

"I got those gardening. I was gardening today." It sounds so strange to me; I've never said those words before in my whole life.

I feel her probing my mind in a strange new way, and when she's done I feel a little like I miss having her inside my head. She becomes such a part of me when she does that, like how a baby is a part of its mother when it's in her womb but after birth it is just a baby by itself, though still connected. She smiles her chevron smile and I know she got the analogy I was thinking of and she liked it. I like pleasing her. She's so cool.

"I am glad that you are gardening Jessie. I understand that our talk inspired you to do so. It is the first step in the healing of the planet. It will help you understand that the planet Earth is a living, breathing organism. It is a living thing that must stay alive for the symbiosis of all life to continue. It is a simple thing that humans forget, and because of that they are the most dangerous threat to Earth."

"I can't believe that humans have to leave the planet some day. It's straight out of some Star Trek episode!"

"Humans of the future are different than in your lifespace," The Granddaughter says with a sigh. "We are connected with the life force of the planet. We feel the planet dying. To live on a dying planet and feel the life force ebb is a difficult thing to do, Jessie. Leaving was the easiest decision our ancestors could have made."

"Your ancestors . . . my future relatives . . . we are all connected in a cosmic way, through time. I feel like it's up to

102

me to start something. Something different. Gardening is my start."

"It is a noble profession in my lifespace."

"On Earth . . . the future Earth . . . what do they do? The Guardians. What do they grow?"

"They grow food, healing herbs, vegetative fuels for our Home Ships, basic nourishment for our people and animals. They provide seeds for our satellite Life Stars, so that our people who have left the planet can grow the foods of Earth. Much of the planet Earth during my lifespace is still healing and very wild. Animals roam freely there. There are some Guardians that tend to the wild places, very brave souls who make sure the native plants are coming in steadily and the invasive ones are not. It is a global restoration project. Everyone who lives on the planet Earth is sworn to protect it.

"Your mother gardened before you, and her mother and grandmother before her. You are continuing the line, Jessie. It is part of your heritage and your destiny. It always was."

The Granddaughter shimmers away yet again, leaving me alone. I feel differently about her now, and about myself, like I am some sort of time traveler's apprentice, learning how to navigate this thing we call humanity.

I hear Dad arrive home from his golf game and he has Keith with him; probably he picked him up at basketball practice on his way home from the club. I get up, and throw on some clothes, and sprint downstairs to say hello.

Chapter Seventeen

The ground is soft and smells like redwood and compost, a mixture my nose has claimed as its own since I was a little kid running around the backyard in my diaper while Mom gardened. Kara hands me another pony pack, those six little plants waiting for their new bed. I was right . . . she ditched school to join us on our planting day.

"These are tomatoes," Kara says, peering at the hard printed label that pokes up through the plastic tray.

"You need to cage those," Mom advises. "Grab one of those cages from over there, will you, Kara?"

Kara hands me a wire frame to set around the plants after I put them into the hole I dug for them. Her black fingernails and smeared dark eye makeup look out of place in this wild corner of our backyard, and I smile at the sight of her. Kara, my tattooed and pierced goth friend, is now the Martha Stewart of continuation school. Who knew.

The day wears on and we become dirtier, more part of the earth than when we started.

"Let's get some lunch," Mom says. We clean up as best we can and hop into her minivan to run to Mooshu You on Hollywood Boulevard. Over noodles and beef we listen to Mom.

"When we first moved here I had big plans for the garden. It's good to see it coming around, some twenty years later."

"Mom always says 'projects that don't get started sit in the corner and pout like a child,'" I quote.

Kara nods. She seems uncomfortable and shifts in her seat, looking paler than usual. I can tell she's holding back tears but Mom doesn't seem to notice as she tells us more about our house when my brother and I were babies. I want to ask Kara why she's sad but now isn't the time.

By three o'clock in the garden it's only me and Kara, finishing up the shade bulbs and pony pack planting. The trees above are filtering a soft golden light that makes the plants glow with a happy kind of peace. We move to the sunny site where we have already planted beans on a big teepee-shaped pole that's been in our garage since I can remember, and now we're building something for potatoes Mom calls "berms." We mound the hay and compost and dirt into piles and shape them.

"You okay?" I ask Kara.

"Me? Fine."

"You sure? Seemed like you were sad at the restaurant."

Kara looks at me, and she does look sad, not her usual defiant self. "I miss my mom."

I don't know what to say. The one thing Kara and I have always had in common was that our mothers were the enemy. Suddenly I've switched sides. I get it, how bizarre it

105

must be for her to see me and my mom palling around after nearly a year of parental bitchfest.

"I told you I was seeing a new therapist . . ." I venture, and she nods. "Well, this is part of that therapy. Don't ask me how it happened, it just did." I feel as if I should say I'm sorry, like somehow I've betrayed her by befriending my own mother.

"It's just a trip," Kara says. "I mean, how you think you have something all hard-wired and figured out, and then suddenly, bam. . .you show up and it's just different." Kara cries, something she's never done in front of me, not even in the shrink ward. She covers her head in her hands and sobs. I put my hand on her shoulder, again not knowing what to say. After a minute she looks up.

"You have this new therapist's number?" she asks with a smile and a sniffle.

I smile, wondering if there's any way to get The Granddaughter to pay a visit to my friend.

"She's not from around here," I say as Kara wipes her eyes carefully to avoid unsmearing her carefully smeared make-up. "And she's pretty hard to get hold of. But I'll mention you to her next time I see her."

"Tell her I could really use her services," Kara says, wiping her nose on her dirty sleeve. Now she has dirt on her nose. I try not to stare at it as she talks. "I mean, we've talked about how messed up life can be, how unfair and all that, but it's so true! My mom just can't handle being around me anymore. I told you she got remarried and moved back east somewhere. She told me she would come get me, you know, after everything settled down and she could find me a therapist and all that, but she hasn't even called me and it's been more than four months. And Dad is never around. I haven't even seen him since last Thursday,

106

when I had my appointment and he drove me. I've gotten rides to the last two, because he never showed up and no one knows where he is. His neighbor thinks he's in Vegas on a gambling spree. It's just so mega . . . here my parents were the biggest problem in my life and now they don't even exist."

Everything Kara says rings a familiar tune in my head. It's exactly where I was heading, I think. This is where I was just a couple of weeks ago . . . Dad was gone at work, and Mom had emotionally checked out and seemed to make a point of working overtime or else being with Keith every chance she got. I feel as if I have been tottering on the edge of a long fall into the abyss and it was The Granddaughter who pulled me away and pointed out my stupidity. I pat the mounded dirt berm and mold the sides into a rounded shape.

"I know what you mean, Kara. I have had that same relationship with my mom, you know. But she's back, I'm back. And we can share her. You can have part of her, too. She really likes you, you know."

Kara smiles up at me. "No one has ever offered to share their mom before, Jess, that's cool. And kind of weird."

"Yeah," I say, and the berm is finally ready to the receive ruddy potato eyes from the brown paper sack.

Chapter Eighteen

Later Mom gives Kara a ride to her therapy appointment with Marsha and I take a shower and a nap.

When I awaken it's dusk, my favorite time of day. I open my eyes to the gloaming time and find not shadows on the wall but Jimmy sitting in a chair beside my bed. I bolt upright.

"What are you doing here?" I move the covers up to hide the fact that I'm not wearing a bra under my tank top.

"I've missed you, Jess," he says, and I can smell him from here, that intoxicating scent of his that reminds me of clean sheets and soap. His long eyelashes droop lazily over his cheeks as he reaches his hands out to me. "I'm so sorry about what I said. I was really mad."

I think I must be dreaming. I look around for a sign of a dream; a ten foot spider dropping in for the kill, a gnome in the corner, a sudden nightfall outside, but everything is normal except that Jimmy, my ex-boyfriend, is sitting in my bedroom. His hand hangs there limply waiting to touch one of my body parts so I move over to him and he pulls my wrist and scoots me onto his knees. Being in that warm safe place makes me remember the good things about Jimmy and I curl up like some lap dog and just breathe in his scent. Somehow in the past two days I had managed to shelve him on the far corner of my mind and forget him, our suspension, and everything that had happened between us. He was a crisis I wasn't able to deal with. I'm convinced, sitting here now, that if he hadn't shown up in my room that I would have never thought of him again. I would have not let myself. I want to cry with relief of being with him but I won't cry anymore, I'm tired of tears and drama. I just want to live my life.

"You must have been a mess," Jimmy says, pulling away and looking me in the face. Actually I'm tanned and freshly scrubbed from my shower. I probably look better than usual, I realize.

"Not really," I say truthfully. "I've been keeping myself busy. How about you?"

His face falls, he's disappointed a little, I can tell. Maybe he's disappointed I didn't try to kill myself over him. But at least he doesn't lie.

"It's been pretty bad," he admits. "I've got the Gestapo on my case, and then, I felt really bad about what I said to you, those horrible words. . . ." He hugs me, and there's something in his voice that is soothing him more than me. *He's here to make himself feel better for being such a dick,* a thought comes into my mind. It seems like it's coming from outside of me, like a small voice only I can hear. I pay attention to the thought and watch Jimmy carefully, wondering if The Granddaughter is sending me the message, but I can't really imagine her using the word "dick." Jimmy strokes my arm and a chill runs through me. I can see he's trying to heat me up. He knows how to chuck his fingers under my chin, how to get me revved up, and damn him, he's doing all those things now. And it's working. His mouth is hot and fevered against mine and I feel myself pulling toward him, as if we are the earth and moon stuck in a weird rhythmic gravitational dance across the galaxy, our bodies molten as we merge across my bed. We are all hands and all tongues and all everything, one together. And that little voice warning me about Jimmy's intentions fades away like a shooting star, with nothing left in its wake, and as the sun disappears slowly outside the window we explode together like new planets born to the universe.

I open my eyes just after midnight and I sit straight up. What the hell? I dreamed I had sex with Jimmy! I touch the pillow beside me; my bed is empty. It seemed so real . . . it even felt real. My window is open, just as it is whenever Jimmy sneaks into my room. My heart thumps wildly . . . I can smell him on my sheets. He was here. It did happen. And then I feel it in my body, know it in my core. This was no dream.

I curl up in fetal position with a sick feeling in the pit of my stomach. Shit, what if I'm pregnant? We didn't even use protection! I can't believe what I've done. I was back on track, I was making big changes to accommodate the future The Granddaughter was talking about. I was even gardening to instill some of the lessons of the future in my unborn child who would save the world! What, a few hot kisses and a couple low strokes and I give it all up? I'm such a slut! I cry until I hear The Granddaughter whisper into the room. She shimmers a dull grayish-blue before me.

"I'm so sorry . . ." I don't know what else to say. Again, as with her last visit, she seems less a real part of this place. Perhaps she's fading, like those photographs in movies about time travel when the stupid person in charge of saving the future does some irreversible harm and all their loved ones fade away in their photographs so that the stupid person knows they've screwed up. I'm the stupid person and The Granddaughter now won't exist.

"You have no need to apologize," The Granddaughter says in her lilting voice.

"But I could be pregnant with Jimmy Becker's child!" I whisper, at least not stupid enough to wake up my parents. I feel like I can't breathe. Is that a symptom of pregnancy? I don't even know. The Granddaughter stares hard at my belly, and I can feel her gaze traveling through me into my womb. I put my hands around my middle, uncomfortable with the sensation.

"You are not pregnant at this time," The Granddaughter says simply.

I can't tell you how relieved I am to hear that. I start crying all over again. Ever since The Granddaughter told me about my future unborn child who would guide the populace as a new kind of messiah, I have felt a need to hold on, to be part of this world. I have equated Jimmy with the death of civilization, and here I am, literally screwing Death. And at the same time, something inside of me died tonight too. I didn't think virginity was any big thing. I'm not really religious, and it seems somehow unnatural to hold onto such a strange concept as virginity. I was only not having sex out of respect for Michael. But now that I gave it up and I'm no longer a virgin. I feel as if I lost something really

111

important, and worse yet, I gave it away so willingly. To Jimmy Becker, someone who maybe doesn't really care about me anyway, who was only at my house to make himself feel better about telling me I wasn't worth the trouble I caused. I sit up and try to stop the tears, remembering how only a few hours ago I had told myself that I was done crying and sick of the drama. I resolve to remember that and I dry my tears, though I'm embarrassed that The Granddaughter can read all of these crazy emotions inside of me.

"You are only human," The Granddaughter says. "Human behavior is more a matter of choices than actions. If you do not wish to continue to participate in this behavior with Jimmy Becker, choose not to."

I can almost feel his warm mouth as she says this and a tiny truth leaks out . . . I did it because I wanted to just do it. Months have been building to that moment, not minutes. As sorry as I am, it was like something I just had to get out of my system. In a way I feel as though I have purged Jimmy from myself. I feel freer of him than I did when I woke up this morning, when he was such a heavy spot on my heart that I could not even admit it. I chose to take Jimmy back in the most intimate way, yet weirdly, I know in my heart that he is no longer my boyfriend. I really am a slut.

"I'm so confused about my life right now," I say out loud.

"You have not changed things in an important way. Do not let yourself worry. I have come to tell you I am pleased about your progress in your new garden. The Earth Guardians of our time will be glad to hear of it."

This is the first time The Granddaughter has acknowledged that she is reporting her visits to me to her Powers That Be, whatever that may look like from her end.

112

"Uh -- could you not mention this little episode tonight to them?" I ask meekly. Her chevron smile causes her to shimmer more brightly.

"It will be our secret," she agrees.

"Um -- and I wanted to ask you something, are you leaving me? I feel your . . . presence . . . isn't as strong anymore." I don't know if that's an offensive question to ask, like asking someone if they've gained weight or something.

"You have grown in your ability to perceive," she tells me. "My mission with you is nearly complete, and the combined energies that is has taken for me to join you on this plane are moving to other sectors. Your perception is accurate. I am fading from this astral plane. But you will see me again. This is not our last meeting."

"Good," I say, glad that she isn't gone from my life yet. In a way she has replaced Michael. Michael would have been really upset that I had sex, and yet The Granddaughter wasn't nearly as disappointed in me as I would have expected.

"Be at peace, Jessie. I will visit again soon," The Granddaughter says as she shimmers away. I snap on the light, deciding to take a shower and maybe begin recording this stuff in my empty journal since there's no way I could go back to sleep now. It's probably time to start writing this crazy crap down anyway, either to show a shrink later when I really go off the deep end or to remind myself of how lost I nearly became in my relationship with Jimmy Becker.

Chapter Nineteen

It's 11:11 in the morning. I stretch and look over at my white painted desk in the corner. The journal I spent half the night working on bulges strangely. I used up a bottle of glue decorating it with rhinestones, broken jewelry, and photo and magazine collages, and a picture I drew of The Granddaughter. Inside I cut and pasted my so-called life with Jimmy Becker. I had started out just making a photo tribute to our relationship, but then added quotes and notes to the pictures of us at the Santa Monica pier, at a big party when we first started dating, at a Green Day concert, at one of his football games at homecoming. Our life in a brightly bound book. That's all I have left of him, but somehow, it's enough.

I get up and wander downstairs and end up with a cup of coffee in the corner chair looking out into our backyard. From here I can see the new garden and I think I want to start a gardening journal too, to keep track of what I plant and what grows and especially, what doesn't. Mom tried to warn me that not everything you plant will grow so basically, don't get too attached until you know a plant will make it. Don't count your corn until it's shucked, she said.

"Morning," I hear Dad say. I smile up at him. He stands by the hassock and moves my slippered feet over so he can sit down. He has his own cup of coffee.

"Did you just wake up too?" I ask him.

"Yeah. Your mom and brother are the early birds. I hate mornings, but when I'm on the job, I have to be on the set before the roosters crow. I've gotta sleep when I can."

We sip our coffee and look out the plate glass window at the typical sunny day. He observes the yard and the new garden. "Like what you've done with the place."

"Thanks. It's been fun, in fact, I need to go out and water."

I suddenly can't wait to get out there to give all of those baby plants their morning shower. I sip faster, planning to grab a Pop Tart from the kitchen and run. As soon as my feet hit the tile Dad clears his throat.

"I saw something unusual last night."

"Oh yeah?"

"Yeah. About 10:30 last night, I was locking up the house, and there was a man on our roof."

I freeze, knowing where this is going.

"Good thing I didn't pull out my rifle and shoot him. My imaginary rifle, since I don't have one. And good thing the motion sensor light went on so I could see who it was before I called the cops. It was Jimmy Becker. Any clue why he was climbing out of your window last night?"

I sink further into the chair, uncomfortable at having to talk to Dad about why there was a boy in my room.

115

"We were saying goodbye to each other. We broke up a few days ago, you know, and it was bad. He came to apologize."

"Can't he use the front door like normal people?"

"He didn't think I'd see him." I don't add that he always climbed up the trellis to get into my bedroom, that my family only ever saw him about a third of the time he was actually in our house.

"That's not okay with me." Dad's normally the cool one, the ex-surf rat who is the anything-goes kind of guy, but I can hear in his voice that he's mad. "This is my house, Jess. I work hard to make it here in LA in a business that can eat you alive. And I'm not working this hard to have my teenaged daughter use it for God-knows-what with her boyfriend. Your room is off-limits to boys, Jess. From this second on. And if I catch Jimmy sneaking in there again I will call the cops and report him for trespassing."

"Okay," I say in a small voice. "I'm sorry."

"That's not all. You've been getting away with murder, in my opinion. First of all, you're suspended. So that means you're under house arrest as well. I saw you hanging out with your friend yesterday like it was summer, not a school day. No more friends over, no phone, nothing but homework and chores until your suspension is over. And normal sleeping hours. I saw your light on at four a.m. when I got up to piss. What the hell is that?"

"I couldn't sleep."

"That's because you slept half the day yesterday. If you need a nap, take a half hour nap and then set your alarm clock and get up. That's it."

"But Michael told mom . . ."

"As far as I know, Michael is no longer part of your life," Dad corrects me. "If you want to see Michael again we can

116

arrange it, but from what I can see, you need to move on, Jess. You were right. Stop labeling yourself the suicide girl and get on with your life. I, for one, am not going to tiptoe around you any more like you're gonna break. You're either in or you're out, the way I see it."

Dad's voice is cracking with emotion and his eyes are damp. My stomach knots with what I've done to him, to make him have to act that way around me like he thinks I'll run to the bathroom with a razor blade again and slit my own wrists. Tears leak out of my eyes but I don't say anything. I can tell Dad has something more on his mind and I want to leave before he can say it, I just can't handle more of this lecture. I lean forward to stand but he holds me back with his arm and looks away, his expression pained.

"I wasn't going to say anything, but . . . I heard you," Dad says in a tight voice. "I heard you and Jimmy, when I came to call you for dinner, and in my own goddamned house I didn't have the balls to break in there and tell that asshole get the hell off my daughter! That's what we've become, a house where everyone is afraid to say anything to anyone because you might do something that would destroy us all! I've had it, Jess! I'm done with that! You are my daughter, this is my house, and these are my rules and you'd better *never* let anything like this happen again!"

I'm so mortified that I can't move, to know that my own Dad heard me having sex in his house. What the hell was I thinking, letting that happen? I'm so angry at myself and Jimmy, too, for coming into my room like that. My entire insides feel like they're twisting inside out.

"I'm sorry, I swear to you Dad, it was the first time, I don't know why . . . why I did that . . . I wish I hadn't. I'm really, really sorry."

"Do we need to--you know, take you to a doctor?" Dad asks. We are both flinching at this question.

"I'm . . . safe, I know for sure." I want to say nothing really happened but I'm not going to lie anymore.

"Okay," Dad sounds as relieved as I felt when The Granddaughter assured me that I wasn't pregnant. It dawns on me that I'm trusting a time traveler with X-ray vision as to whether or not I'm going to have my ex-boyfriend's baby, but I decide that I've trusted her this far and if I start to doubt her that I may truly end up in the mental ward again.

"Are you really broken up this time? Because I forbid you to see him anymore, Jess. Your mom thinks he walks on water but I can see him for the horny jock that he is. That boy is nothing but trouble. You're too good for him, Jess. You have too much to offer to get caught up with that kind of shallow person. I knew a million of them in high school."

These words surprise me, and I'm grateful for them. I put down my coffee cup and reach over and hug Dad. We hold each other and cry a little and then sit back sniffling.

"I'm really done with Jimmy, Dad. And I'm sorry -- sorry I disrespected you. I didn't mean to. It wasn't planned."

"I can't talk about it any more. It's too damn hard. You know where I stand." Dad sips his coffee and I lean up to go.

"I've missed you, Jess. The real you. Please come back to me," Dad says unexpectedly.

"I'm right here," I tell him. He pats me on the knee as I get up, my emotions a wreak.

"Good. And one more thing . . . if you don't get on top of that stinking pile of laundry in your room, you'll be grounded until your senior graduation."

118

"I hear you," I say, smiling and wiping the rest of my tears. Normally him saying something like that would piss me off and I'd be rebellious about it, but he's right . . . that pile does stink, and besides, wouldn't it be the coolest thing to go back to school Monday wearing clean clothes for once?

Chapter Twenty

In my room clean clothes are stacked on my bed, my dresser, my desk, and on the floor. I ran out of room in my drawers and closet an hour ago and now am faced with an inescapable fact: I have too many clothes. Me, the nothing-to-wear girl who hasn't had a clean shirt since September. I sigh and look hopelessly at the piles. It's time to weed through the whole thing, including the ones I already put away, but I'm not feeling so hot. Dad decided he's cleaning out the garage so on our "breaks," his from garage organizing and mine from laundry hell, we've been meeting and watching HGTV to inspire us while eating too much Ben and Jerry's. I leaf through a pile of folded T-shirts. The top one is from Lazy J Ranch. I got it when I went to camp there with Molly when we were nine but the shirt just now fits me; I used it as a nightshirt before. Nostalgia aside, I would never wear it. I kick the empty laundry basket in front of me and drop it in. This is going to take the rest of the day, and it's that warm-sun-on-the-walls time of day when I usually nap. I remember what Dad says and I set my alarm for one hour from now and lean back to rest my head on my pillows, thinking about The Granddaughter. I wonder how she can visit me. Do we really have that capability now, as she says? A part of ourselves we haven't tapped into yet? I remember Michael telling me once that we don't use our entire brains and that some people use even less than that. I don't get this whole being human thing. Why are we here? What is life, what is death? Where is the meaning? Sometimes it just seems like one of Dad's movies, a big set where we go around saying our lines and acting out our parts . . . but for what? Is it for the applause at the end of the show? What if no one is watching?

These and other creepy thoughts plague me until my eyes close, and the creepy thoughts spiral into darkness.

After my nap I'm back in the garden checking on the plants. I hear strange crackling noises behind the fence. A shadow blocks the five o'clock sun slanting through the boards. I can tell from the footfalls that it isn't The Granddaughter, but who is it?

"Jess!" A voice calls me. It's Jimmy. My heart surges. What's he doing here? It dawns on me I've only broken up with him in my mind. I haven't actually told him yet that we're through. In fact, as far as he knows, we're moving into a really fun new place in our rekindled relationship . . . having sex.

I wedge open a broken board and Jimmy squeezes through the fence, looking around like a spy on a mission.

"I had to see you," he says, kissing me on the lips. "Last night was . . . amazing. I can't stop thinking about you!" He gropes for me and starts mashing against me. There's that amazing scent of his and--yes, there go the eyelashes. Damn him. My body starts its own little dance against his.

"What are you doing here?" I ask, deja vu in my head.

"I had to sneak out. I've tried to call you but your dad . . . he's trippin'. He won't let me talk to you!"

"He knows about us, Jimmy," I say in a quiet voice. "He knows we had sex. He heard us!"

Jimmy looks appropriately horrified at this news. "No way! He must be bugging out!"

"I'm in lock down," I say, looking away from his eyelashes. I notice the mint plant looks taller than it did this morning. Wow.

"Me too. My dad thinks I'm taking out the trash, so I can't stay. Is there any place . . ." he looks around and I know what he wants. What's he expecting, some Bedouin tent to miraculously appear so we can go inside and do it? What a jerk.

"No," I say firmly.

"Too bad," he says, playing me with his hands, rubbing me to get me horny. I grab his hands in mine and push them away.

"Don't start something you can't finish."

"Who says we can't finish?" he asks, trying to put his hands back on me. That sick feeling I had earlier after eating too much ice cream comes back. Jimmy makes my stomach turn.

"I said no, Jimmy, my dad's really disappointed in me. I feel bad about it too, and because of that and everything else . . . I think we should stop seeing each other."

"You? You're sorry for what you've done? That doesn't sound like you, Jess."

"What are you saying?"

"I'm saying, that's the whole thing about you. You try to kill yourself but instead of being all sorry and whiny about it you were in everyone's face. Almost like you were proud of it or something. You weren't just some messed-up loser, you were like this . . . chick on the edge. Like daring death to take you or something. Now you're backing down from what you want because your dad found out you're not a virgin anymore? That's not you, Jess."

"It's me now, Jimmy. That's what I'm saying. And I'm not backing down from what I want. This is what I want. I want to break up with you. You're not good for me anymore."

"Wait a sec . . . you're the one who got me in trouble! I'm suspended from school because you asked me to come get you in the middle of the night! How can you be breaking up with me?"

"You're just mad cuz I finally screwed you and now you want more and you can't have it." All these feelings are fountaining up, and words I've waited to say puke themselves out.

"I can't believe you!" Jimmy says, his face flushing with anger. "You were lucky to even get a date with me! So lucky! My friends told me you were all wrong, but no, I gave you a chance! I even let myself love you in spite of what the whole world said about you! I was wrong, you are a jacked-up loser. You'll never have it as good as you would with me . . . you are a crazy bitch!"

I watch Jimmy's little rampage and wonder what my next line is in the script of life. I shrug. I feel like calling out "line!" to the invisible director of my personal B-Movie.

123

Maybe someone would write me a brilliant comeback that would leave the audience laughing and begging for more. There's nothing though, just an empty hole in my heart where Jimmy Becker's love used to be.

"Sorry," I say to Jimmy. "Don't think you didn't mean anything to me. You really did. You meant a lot to me, Jimmy. I really loved you."

A strange nasally sigh comes from Jimmy that reminds me of Michael's unhappy noise and he leaves quickly through the broken fence slat. I'm glad I got to tell him that I loved him. I'm glad I didn't stoop to his level and resort to name calling. I did love him. My body still loves him, apparently, and I can feel a residual burn in all the places he just touched me.

My imaginary movie director didn't give me a comeback line so the one I came up with was as good as I could give. I finish watering the plants and head up to the house, picking my way up the rock-lined path.

Chapter Twenty-one

Now it's dark out. Mom is sitting on my bed. We are going through the last pile of clothes and have filled three trash bags of leftover stuff to donate to charity, including some old stuffed animals, books, dolls, and toys. She says she's hitting Keith's room next.

"How about this," Mom says, holding up a brown halter with pink lace trim.

"Keep. I bought that at the beginning of the school year and only wore it once!"

"It's been in the dirty laundry forever. Funny how that stuff piles up."

"Never again," I say, amazed at how many cool clothes I have that I forgot about. It's like having a whole new wardrobe.

"This?" Mom asks. A black tank with spaghetti straps.

"It goes under the brown one. There's a white one, too, somewhere. I wear them all together."

"Well, no wonder you have so many clothes if you wear three shirts at once!" Mom laughs. This is fun, I think, hanging out with Mom and talking about clothes. I laugh too.

"This?"

Mom holds up a pink and black splotched Green Day shirt from the concert I went to with Jimmy. My throat clutches.

"Keep," I whisper. Mom looks at me strangely. "Billy Joe is so cute!" I add, to lighten things up.

"Who?" Mom asks.

I point to the dark-haired band member on the front of the shirt.

"He's wearing eyeliner like Kara's," she says and she shrugs and puts the folded shirt in the drawer that's been pulled onto the bed. It's nearly full.

"Everything in this drawer is a keeper. But your dad is having a big yard sale Saturday. He put an ad in the paper. You should try to sell some of your old clothes. Then the Salvation Army is coming on Monday and you can give the rest to charity. You may make some money and clear some room in here."

"Okay. I'll set up a little table. I have some jewelry and vintage stuff I could add."

"I'll let your dad know he has some competition."

I'm actually excited about the prospect of hanging out in the front yard all day selling my stuff, making money. I can work on my tan too. Mom gets up and starts to go.

"Mom," I say, stopping her. "I broke up with Jimmy."

"You told me, earlier this week. Remember?"

"No, I mean I really did it, today."

Mom sits back down. "How'd it go?"

"It was rough. He called me a couple of names. But I told him I had really loved him and so that's how I ended it, no matter what he said."

"I'm sorry," Mom says, touching my arm. "It's hard to have a broken heart." She puts her arm around me and I lean my head against her.

"Men." I say.

Mom laughs. "Want to get some ice cream?"

I shake my head quickly. "I think I'll stay here and figure out how much to sell my stuff for."

"Okay, I'll warn your dad," Mom releases me and leaves. So Dad didn't tell her, I think. I can really move on from this without hashing out the whole de-virginity thing. I'm grateful. I return the drawer to the dresser and I'm about to open the nearest bag when I catch The Granddaughter faintly shimmering into the corner of the room. She looks pale somehow, like a memory of herself.

"Hi!" I say, like I'm seeing an old friend. "So much has happened since I last spoke to you . . ."

"I am aware of it, yes," The Granddaughter says weakly. "You have cut the thread of emotion that attached you to Jimmy Becker. That is good news for your future relatives."

"Is that how it works?" I ask, wondering at this information. "That there's an invisible thread that attaches you to someone, and when your relationship is over, it's gone? Because that's exactly how it felt, like it snapped."

"The thread of human attachment is always present, even between people who have a relationship but have never met, such as yourself with my mother, for example."

"Your mother?" I say, blanking out. Somehow The Granddaughter always seemed like some science-experiment spawn, and I'd always thought of her as being hatched in a fish nursery or something. Her sweet smile

127

gives away the fact that she knows what I'm thinking, as always.

"I was birthed the way all humans have been birthed throughout the ages. We do have other ways of creating humans, but in my lifespace natural childbirth is still the most popular way of being born."

"Other ways? You mean cloning and stuff like that?" I ask, loving that I get to know the inside scoop of future millennia.

"Stuff like that, yes," The Granddaughter says vaguely, trying out my slang. "Things that would be outside your comprehension in this lifespace."

I love it when she uses that word.

"Humans have changed much since your lifespace, Jessie. Especially those no longer living on Earth. And part of that change is due to you and the choices you'll make in the next few years of your living."

"What if I had gotten pregnant and had Jimmy Becker's child?" I muse out loud.

"We would not be speaking together now."

"And same thing if I'd killed myself, you would never have been born."

"Correct."

Wow, I think. Every action we make as humans on earth affects some future action. It's a hard thing to get my head around that concept and it makes me feel both small and huge at the same time. I'm this little tiny dot on the universal radar, just another human living her life, and yet everything I do will affect those who come after me. Crazy.

"I have a gift for you," The Granddaughter says. "It is not an object . . ." She's reading my mind cuz I was just thinking how cool it would be to get some present from the future, like some jewelry or something-- "but it is something that will help you live your life." She reaches toward me and holds my hands in hers and a thick buzzing sensation fills my body, my hands go white-hot and have that funky glow-in-the-dark mark on them that they had when she touched me on the arm when I first met her. I feel something get dumped into me, something I can't describe but it reminds me of reading a book, how as you read each page you get more information. And then I realize, she is giving me information. She's sending me knowledge. She lets go and my knees feel weak and I sit down on my bed, woozy.

"What is it?" I ask when I can speak again.

"It is . . . awareness."

"Awareness?"

"It is a gift for you to know when you are on the right life path. This gift will help you stay focused. It will be there to guide you, since I will no longer be able to guide you. Soon I will leave you but this essence of myself will stay behind."

"How does it work?"

"When you are on the right path, certain things will happen that will be markers for that path. You may call it coincidence, but in my lifespace we know it to be a guiding force."

"Is it like . . . a God thing or something?"

"It is your purpose and your destiny. Both of those qualities have been connected to the idea of God before. You may call it whatever you wish. It is the way the future, as you call it, is molded."

"I'm not sure I understand," I say, wishing I could figure out exactly what the gift is.

"You will understand. You will feel something similar to my presence at first when the gift is working. Trust your instincts, Jessie. Do what your inner voice says is correct."

Her words remind me of Obi-Wan telling Luke to use the force.

"I'm not sure. . ." I say and Mom is standing there in the doorway, looking around the room just as The Granddaughter vanishes. She drops a large box on the ground by the laundry basket.

"What are you not sure about, Jess? If you're not sure, sell it. You probably won't need it."

Mom is talking garage sales and I'm talking about the fate of the world to an invisible being.

"It's . . . stuffy in here or something." Mom walks right through The Granddaughter's still-bluish space and heads for the window and opens it. "I brought some things from the garage to see if you want to sell any of them. I know, that's crazy, I should have had you come down and look but you should see what your dad has done out there, it looks like a thrift shop . . ."

She pushes the big box toward me and pulls out my old dance shoes, my roller skates, and an old mini-trampoline from my two month "workout" period. I'm still confused about what The Granddaughter was trying to say when Mom looks at me.

"You okay?" she asks, putting her hand on my forehead. It's as if we've both forgotten that she hasn't really touched me in nearly a year until just a couple weeks ago. "You look . . . different. Glowy. I don't know."

"I'm just confused," I say honestly.

"It's hard to decide what to keep and get rid of," Mom says. "Maybe you need a break. Want to take a walk or watch some TV or something?"

"Walk," I say, thinking the fresh air might do my muddled brain some good.

Chapter Twenty-two

At the yard sale people from every walk of life show up. I'm sitting in an old lawn chair and my clothes are selling well, mostly because of the sign we put on Sunset that points arrows toward our house (my idea). The cool and fashionable from Hollywood that stroll our way aren't disappointed, especially when they see my vintage collection from when I was in seventh grade and thought that the forties was the best decade ever. I'm so over that now, though. I'm raking in the dough selling my thrift shop boutique clothes.

Dad has tools for sale, and he's doing pretty well himself selling off his cheaper tools since he inherited his dad's good tools a few years ago when Grandpa died. All the men in the neighborhood crowd around Dad's workshop, gleaming hammers and screwdrivers oiled to a shine and displayed like jewels on the old card table. They discuss things like drywall and nailgun technique. Boring.

I notice another element, those who live just near us; the dog walking people with the new gangly puppy, the old guy, Mr. Finney, from down the street where I used to meet Jimmy, the lady across the street who is always spying out her curtains at our comings and goings. They aren't shopping our yard sale. They are here to look at the Suicide Girl, to get a glimpse of our street's craziest person. Mom seems oblivious but I can tell by the way they are looking over at me out of the sides of their eyes. I smile and say hi as pleasantly as I can, but I feel uncomfortable in a way I can't explain. It makes me think about what The Granddaughter said about paying attention to my inner voice, and right now my inner voice is telling me that I don't want to get attention for the bad or crazy shit that I do. It's embarrassing to be that person. I always thought I thrived on being wild and different but now I'm not so sure. Calm and centered seems like as good a plan as any.

We're wrapping up at three and I'm putting what's left of my junk in a bag for charity. Kara shows up. I look over at my dad.

"Can I talk to Kara while I put my stuff away?" I ask. Dad seems shocked that I'm asking permission, but he recovers quickly and says "I suppose, but then you're inside finishing your homework." He sounds like such a dad I'm actually kind of proud of him.

Kara helps me clean up and I give her a couple outfits that are left over (she still likes the forties). Soon we are alone sitting in the garage waving off the latecomers.

"You seem like you're doing really well," she comments, picking at her black ripped tights.

"I am. But I'm nervous about going back to school on Monday."

"I don't blame you."

"And I have a Michael appointment, so I have that to deal with too."

"I thought you were only going there once a month now?"

"Mom's insisting. One more."

"Michael probably misses you."

"He probably thinks I need him."

"Don't you?"

"Not anymore."

Mom doesn't agree; that's why she arranged for me to see Michael once more after my first day back at school. I think of The Granddaughter's gift and realize for the first time how much it will help me in my whole life, not just at this hard and messed up time of my lifespace, as she calls it. I mean, mostly it's adults who see shrinks. The Granddaughter's gift could help me avoid the expense of psychotherapy forever. Cool.

"I'd be afraid to leave my therapist," Kara admits. "I mean, I count on Marsha. I'm used to talking things out with her."

"That's how I felt about Michael but now I sort of think that I've been over-analyzing every detail of my life and not really living my life, you know what I mean?"

Kara considers this. "I guess, but I'd still be afraid. You're so brave, Jessie."

I laugh at this. Brave is what I thought I was. I thought I tried to kill myself because I was brave enough to test the edge, but now I realize that I was actually the world's

133

biggest coward. I remember Buffy the Vampire Slayer telling her little sister Dawn, "the hardest thing to do in this world is to live in it," and now I totally get what she meant. Living life is way harder than chickening out and offing yourself. Of course Buffy said those words right before she sacrificed her own life to save the world (again). What else are you going to say before you take the swan dive to Goodbye Forever?

"I have a lot of homework to make up, Kara," I say. "I was wondering if you wanted to start studying together after school sometimes. Maybe get a mocha and hit the books."

"Study?" Kara stares at me blankly. Somehow in our drama about ourselves and our shrinks and our hospitals school fell out of the top ten things we need to think about, for both of us. School for me was all about Jimmy and just getting through the day with my head held high in defiance for anyone who had a problem with what I tried to do.

"School's going to be kind of hard for me, since Jimmy and I broke up."

"You really broke up with Jimmy?"

"For good, this time. And now going back there will be awkward. It might help if I knew we could get our homework done together. Jimmy's friends used to do his homework for him and I'd just call him for the answers. Now I have to study for real."

"Well, sorry about Jimmy," Kara says. "Weird I never met him. At least you never, you know . . . did the nasty with him."

"I did."

"You did?"

"Yes."

We both let that sink in and then Kara uses some of the tact taught to her by her many shrinks.

"And how did that make you feel?"

We both crack up.

Chapter Twenty-three

When Mom's minivan pulls up into the high school parking lot on Monday we arrive promptly before our seven a.m. meeting with Mr. Hicks, Principal from Hell. Mom has a determined look on her face as she scoots Keith off to class. Dad slouches with his hands in his pockets, probably reliving in his mind his own days on a high school campus. I'm wearing a totally cute (and clean) outfit which helps me feel a little better about the early birds on campus who are staring at me while pointing and whispering.

Mr. Hicks' office is cold as he unlocks it and escorts us in, having just arrived himself. Mom and I sit down on the couch and Dad takes the chair by Mr. Hicks' desk. Mr. Hicks takes the large latched envelope that Dad hands him and checks off my homework assignments.

"Today you have an opportunity to begin your life fresh, Jessica," Mr. Hicks begins. Dad clears his throat.

"Jessie just wants to get an education at this school, and she's entitled to that," he says.

"Yes, and here she is, messing up her life and the lives of our other students ..." Dad raises his hand to stop him.

"Jessie has not done one thing wrong on this campus," Dad says in a level voice. "And you would not have even known about the incident involving Jimmy Becker if Alex Becker wasn't an old college buddy of yours. It was completely inappropriate of you to suspend her, Mr. Hicks, and I feel you owe her an apology and I request that her suspension be removed from her permanent record."

Mr. Hicks' mouth opens and closes. "She is completely out of control ..." he sputters, pointing at me.

"Jessie's behavior regarding Jimmy Becker happened away from campus and not during school hours, and it is a matter of parental concern, not something the school should have been involved in," Dad presses on. "I'm sure the school board would agree with me if it came down to it. It's a simple matter, Mr. Hicks. You made a mistake and you owe my daughter and my wife and I an apology. We will let the matter drop if you do as we have asked."

Obviously Mr. Hicks' morning isn't going as planned. I look up and see Jimmy and his dad standing outside the principal's office waiting for their back-to-school meeting.

"Jimmy's suspension too," I pipe up as he looks away from me. "You need to take it off his record."

Mr. Hicks turns red and looks embarrassed. "Suspensions stay in the school records only and don't go on the permanent records, but you should know I'm only trying to help you with your girl. She's obviously a very

137

troubled kid and I thought I might be doing her a favor, to have her face the consequences of her actions."

"We'll handle the discipline," Dad says firmly. "And Jessie is not any more troubled than any other kid. Yes, she made mistakes last year. Yes, she's paid for it. But she's grown as a person since then. You need to remember she has had to come back here day after day after attempting suicide. Every kid at this school talks about her or has an opinion about her. Every teacher too. And still she's managing to keep her grades in the B and C range, and she's trying to have a social life. And then people like you are out gunning for her, waiting for her to mess up again. You may as well just give her a nudge toward the cliff while you're at it, Mr. Hicks. You're making it that much harder for her to be okay."

Dad has an edge in his voice like when he flipped out on me the other morning, and Mom looks surprised to see Dad in his action-hero suit, welding his light saber against the bad guy to protect me.

"I don't mean to," Mr. Hicks says, looking up and noticing his friend, Jimmy's dad, standing outside the glass door. He nods toward him. "All right, then, I apologize," Mr. Hicks says breezily. "I will let you handle the discipline of Jessica, and I expect you to allow an open line of communication between yourselves and the school should anything come up that I think merits a warning."

"We came here last April when Jessie returned from the hospital and told you we were available to discuss any problems," Mom says. "We meant it. We need to stay informed."

"Very well," Mr. Hicks says. He shakes Mom and Dad's hands and we go.

"Alex," Dad says to Mr. Becker.

"Hello, Greg," Mr. Becker says back. Mr. Becker pushes past me and I end up face to face with Jimmy. He looks at me and then looks away and follows his dad into the office. When he lowers his eyelashes my insides give a sigh but I walk on.

The rest of the day doesn't improve. I'm now the school's biggest Slut of the Week, and my story has escalated into we got suspended for having sex at school in the girl's locker room during lunch. I keep my head down and try to avoid eye contact. Molly and Cristabelle already cornered me once in the hallway and I got right in their faces and told them to leave me the hell alone. It embarrassed them so they backed off. Suddenly the punk girls from school have a new interest in me and they are actually nice and invite me to sit with them at lunch, although I kind of find their nose and eyebrow rings distracting when they chew. I sort of know one of them, the T.A. from my science class. Suzi is a little more mellow and a little more friendly and a little less pierced than the others. She's a punk-rock science geek and I like her.

"The science club is doing a project, you should check it out," she says, handing me a goldenrod sheet from the stack in her backpack. It's a flier for the club's school-wide science fair. I shrug.

"Maybe."

"You get extra credit for science. It's an easy way to raise your grade."

Science is my worst subject, worse even than math, and Jimmy was the one helping me through it. I look more closely at the paper. The clip art is of microscopes and magnifying glasses and a caption that reads E=MC2. I wonder about what that means, what it really means. That buzzy Granddaughter feeling hits me and I stare at the flier with renewed interest. Someone is giving me information. There is a reason for it. E=MC2 has something to do with it. This is part of the path. This is The Granddaughter's gift, in action.

"Okay, I'll do it," I say to Suzi. "Can you help me get started, though? I have no clue about this stuff."

Suzi smiles. "Sure. Meet me today at the science club meeting after school in room 214 and I'll give you the entry packet."

I nod, in wonder at myself. What the hell? Science club, me? I would never in a million years have looked twice at that flier if The Granddaughter hadn't given me her gift. I wonder what I'm in for as I try get through the rest of my day, incident-free.

Chapter Twenty-four

After school Suzi and I hang out. She's super short and she'd hate it if she knew everyone thought she was cute. Her science geek friends seem happy to see her when we show up at the science club meeting. We're the only two cool looking people there but everyone else is nice to me, so maybe they don't know about my sordid story or if they do, they don't care.

"So this is all you need, to fill out these forms. I'll give you a hand with your hypothesis and stuff like that since it can be intimidating if you haven't done it before," Suzi says as she hands me a thick packet of papers. I notice she wears a silver ring on every finger. "Do you know what you want to do your project on?"

"What do you mean?" I ask, pulling my fingers through my blue-black hair. I'm starting to wonder what I'm doing here again and I remember The Granddaughter feeling so I try to focus.

"Your project. Any ideas? You're only about a week behind . . . you still have time to put something great together."

"It will come to me," I say, hoping it will be true. I point to the E=MC2 on the cover page. "What is this, anyway? Can I do a project on that?" For some reason it still hits a chord with me.

"That's Einstein's theory on how the speed of light is constant so that means time and space can change," Suzi says thoughtfully, as if explaining to a kindergartner. "It opens up a theory that time travel is possible."

"You mean, like in *Back to the Future*?" I reference that old movie my dad and I used to watch together all the time, but I'm thinking of The Granddaughter's voyage here from her 'lifespace.'

"Yes, sort of like that, except that the theory is that you can only go forward in time, not back."

"Not yet," I mutter, wondering what The Granddaughter would say if she could hear that. I get the sense that we are truly in the infancy of our scientific development here on Earth.

"Well, Einstein is pretty complicated. You might want to start with something simpler. Even Newton's law. . ."

"Is that the one that says that for every action there is a reaction?" I ask, wondering how I know that. Maybe information sort of leaks into you when you are sitting in class, even if you aren't paying attention.

"That's the gist of it," Suzi says with a laugh. "Even that one would be easier to do a project on. You're just joining in, so stick with something you know. Try to come up with something that you care about."

I think about that for a second as Suzi gets broadsided by a tall skinny-armed kid who picks her up and swings her around. I hear him saying her name and her laughing and I think of my plants, my garden at home. Maybe I can do something with the plants? I gather up the information and look at the clock. I suddenly remember that I have a four o'clock appointment with Michael.

"Oh my God, I have to leave," I tell Suzi. "I forgot about a doctor's appointment!"

"You had a whole week off and you have a doctor's appointment now?" she asks with a grin.

"You know about that?" I ask, blushing.

"Everyone knows about that," Suzi says, and the few kids nearby who are eavesdropping nod. My face turns even redder.

"Well . . . don't believe everything you hear," I finally say.

"I never do. That's why I want to be a scientist."

"Good. I'll see you tomorrow."

"Call me tonight and we'll talk about your project."

"Okay!" I hand her my cell and she enters her number. I put the cell and the packet of papers in my backpack and head out the door toward the bus stop.

I'm ten minutes late to Michael's office. He looks surprised to see me somehow. I think he thought I wasn't coming. He pulls my folder from under his desk blotter and takes the cap off his pen.

"Hi," I say, and I am glad to see him in that "hey homey" kind of way.

"You look great, Jessie. I see you've been working on that tan. Have a seat."

I sit in a different chair, the one right across from his desk usually reserved for those intense family meetings. His eyebrows shoot up a tiny bit but he doesn't say anything.

"So how have you been coping with everything?" Michael asks, pen poised.

"Great."

He leans in, waiting for me to elaborate. "Good. What issues have been coming up for you in the last week?"

"All kinds. Everything. It's been a real ride, being suspended and now going back to school."

"I'm sure it has," Michael agrees, settling into his role as shrink. "Tell me more."

I look at him, his buttoned up Izod shirt and cashmere sweater, and I take in his dark and oppressive leather and wood office, those high windows and short lamp cords. I just don't feel up to this at all any more. This guy really helped me come back from the dead, but now I want to be at the science club meeting with Suzi, I want to do homework tonight with Kara, and I want to get back to my garden to water my plants and write in my journal and talk to The Granddaughter before she leaves me forever. I can do none of those things in this office. Talking is not living.

"There's a million things we could talk about, Michael. I had sex for the first time . . . with Jimmy, and then I broke up with him. It was like something I needed to get out of my system, but my dad found out. We had to go through this huge emotional thing and I feel bad for letting my dad down. But I also had a week off to discover some things I didn't know about myself, and I am starting to take charge of my own life. I had clean clothes for school today because I did my own laundry. I made some money selling my stuff I didn't want anymore. I met a new friend and joined the science club. Mom and I hung out and actually had fun

144

together. But most importantly, I just lived my life for the first time, without thinking every second about what I would tell you. Without always thinking about what I did last year." I pause and Michael's poised pen hovers over my file.

"That's a good start, Jessie. Just living your life is a healthy approach, but you need to be able to watch for signs of a setback. You know we've gone over it . . ."

". . . And over it and over it, and you know what? I'm not depressed. I'm not sure I ever was. It was just like I couldn't stand being myself anymore. Or like life wasn't interesting enough, or I didn't care enough to be here. It was like this fog of apathy, not 'oh I hate myself I'm going to kill myself.' It was just -- something to do. I can't explain it, Michael. I'm sick of living almost a year of my life regretting what I did. It's my label now and that's punishment enough."

"Okay, I can respect that." Michael stops and scribbles some notes. He flips a few pages, stops at one, squints at it, and taps his pen on his desk before looking up at me again.

"Once we discussed something I'd like to revisit. You said you were approached by a time traveling being who claimed to be a descendent of yours. What is happening there? Have you experienced any more of these visitations?"

I hesitate. I have never lied to Michael. I have exaggerated to shock him or push his buttons back when we played the Therapist Game, but I have never lied. But I can't give up The Granddaughter. She has given me so much, and has guided me on a level that brought me a new understanding of who I want to be.

"I know I said that. And I sort of believed it at the time. But that happened after I woke up from a nap, before I was really awake. I'm pretty sure I dreamed that. It seemed so

145

real but now I think it was just one of those dreams you can't wake up from."

"You showed me a mark on your arm where you said the being touched you. . ."

"I was confused. Like I said, it seemed real at the time." I drop the subject as Michael writes.

"I see," Michael says. Again he flips through the notes in my file. He peers up at me.

"So you had sexual intercourse with your boyfriend." He sounds disappointed.

"I wish I hadn't, but I did."

"Your father found out?"

"Yes, but like I said, I wish I hadn't done it. Now we're broken up anyway. Permanently."

"Did you see a doctor about potential pregnancy or sexually transmitted diseases?"

"Yes, and I'm fine," I lie, thinking, how do I know The Granddaughter isn't a doctor? I've never actually asked her what her profession is, if they even have healing jobs like that in the über-future. Michael scribbles furiously in the file.

"Uh -- you referred to your mother as 'Mom' earlier. You have only called her Mother in our sessions since we began. Is there a reason for the change?" Michael asks.

I'm surprised. "I did?"

"Yes."

"I hadn't noticed that. I guess I like her better now. Like I said, we're getting along," I say, feeling uncomfortable about Michael's pre-conceived ideas about my relationship with my family. It seems so invasive, that this man who we pay all of this money to holds in his mind a twisted version of our family dynamics. It kind of creeps me out.

"Look," I say as he writes, a habit that's now starting to bug me. "We agreed, and you even suggested, that I fly solo for awhile, right? And then mom set up this appointment for me cuz she thought I'd have trouble my first day back at school. But I didn't ask to come back here, Michael." I take a deep breath, wondering how to say the words that are jumping to the surface. I blurt it out. "In fact, I only agreed to come here to tell you that I'm done with this place. I want to quit therapy, as of right now. For good. No more checking in, monthly appointments, none of it. Just done."

Michael puts down his pen. "I see." If he's disappointed I can't tell. If he's happy for me I can't see that either. He's a stone, calm and serene and great at hiding his emotions when he has to. Right now he has to.

"Do your parents know this decision you've made?"

"They'll support me on it," I say confidently. "But I don't think I'll be needing you anymore." I decide to shut up now because I meant that to sound like he was successful doing his job because I'm okay, but it came out more like 'screw you'.

"I'm going to support you in your decision, Jessie," Michael says stiffly. "And if you want to stay longer today and talk, that's fine with me, you still have some time left on the clock. But if not that's fine by me too. I want you to do what you feel like doing."

I stand up quickly. "You've been great for me, Michael. You were totally there when I needed you. But I really want to get home and take care of my new garden and get my homework done. I have a science fair project coming up and I want to get a jump on that too."

Michael stands up and reaches his hand across the desk. I come around the desk and give him a hug.

147

"Thank you so much," I say. When we part I see a tiny spec of emotion in his eyes. He'll miss me too, I know.

"I'll contact your parents and let them know your decision. And if things get intense for you feel free to call me."

"Things are intense for me right now. But that's just life." I pick up my backpack and hurry downstairs. When I hit the sunlit sidewalk and hear the roar of traffic off Santa Monica Boulevard I feel free. I put on my shades and hurry to the bus stop, hoping I won't have to wait too long.

Chapter Twenty-five

We have a normal family dinner again and I find myself wishing Dad wouldn't take his next job. Now that Mom is coming home earlier from work, we're like those families on commercials where everyone sits down and passes big steaming bowls of food around. It's cool. We're sitting around listening to one of Dad's stories about a mishap on his last set when the doorbell rings.

"I'll get it!" Keith yells, jumping up and tearing for the door. I expect it to be one of his grimy little freshman friends but I hear Kara's voice and remember our homework date.

"There's Kara," I say, and I start to get up. Mom puts her hand over mine.

"Wait," Mom says, and she looks at Dad. "We wanted you to know that Michael called and told us what you did today."

149

"Are you okay with that?" I ask, alarmed. It dawns on me that they hadn't wanted to discuss it at dinner in front of Keith and that's why they'd waited for this stolen moment.

"I'm proud of you, honey," Dad says.

Mom nods. "It's up to you. I like who you are becoming, Jess."

For some reason that makes me get choked up and I smile but the corners of my mouth tremble.

"Thanks," I say, hugging Mom. Dad pats my back. Kara walks in and stands uncertainly in the doorway. Keith pushes past her and sits back down to finish his dessert.

"Hey," I say to Kara. "Want to study in my room or in the office?"

"Let's go to your room. Hi," she says shyly to my parents.

"Hello, Kara. Do you want a brownie? I baked a double pan."

"Um . . . sure. Thanks." Kara takes the brownie that Mom hands her in a napkin. I grab a second one and we go in the kitchen and each get a small glass of milk before going upstairs to my room.

We eat and wash the chocolate off our hands before even cracking our books. I don't have too much homework but I want to start working on my science fair project. I pull the packet out of my backpack, careful not to upset the other books that teeter recklessly on the chair beside me.

"What do you think?" I ask Kara. "I want to do something on the science fair about the garden."

Kara thinks a minute. "I have an idea. I saw this funky movie at my ex-step-mom's house about how this guy wrote words on these water bottles and then afterward froze the water and photographed the ice up close. The ones with nice words like 'Love' and 'Peace' had these cool snowflake-looking patterns in them, but the ones marked with words like 'War' and 'Hate' had these ugly marks when it was photographed."

I stare at her, wondering what she's saying. "How does it work?" I ask.

"Well, I can't remember exactly but I think the water was frozen first and then some thoughts or words were sent to the water. Or sometimes classical music was played. Either way the ones with harmonious thoughts made these cool bright crystals and the ones with negative thoughts just made weird patterns."

I wonder how I can do something similar. "I can't really freeze and photograph water. But maybe I can do something similar with plants?"

"Well, you still have seeds leftover, right? Maybe you could plant them and be nice to some of them and mean to others and measure the difference in their growth or something?"

I laugh at the idea of being mean to a plant. In fact, the idea of it sort of bothers me, but it sounds interesting. "That might work! Do you think I have time?"

"The project isn't due for five more weeks," Kara reads, pointing to the flier.

"That's enough time to measure the differences in growth, right? I mean, it's only been a week and our garden is growing already."

Kara smiles and her black-rimmed eyes brighten. "I've never had a garden before."

"You have one now. And you'll be eating vegetables from it soon!"

"I'm not a huge vegetable fan but who cares," Kara says with a laugh.

"I'll write up the thesis while you do your homework."

151

Kara takes the goldenrod flier from my hand to read it more closely. "Hey, I got this exact same thing at school. You know that I would be going to Hollywood High if I weren't in continuation school, right?"

"Yeah, you'd be a senior. I know."

"Well, maybe we can work on this together. This flier says you can have a partner."

The Granddaughter sensation comes over me at the prospect of working with Kara on the project, especially since we share the garden too. "I'll call Suzi and ask her if it's okay, but I have a feeling it will be. She's the science geek I told you about."

"I never thought you'd be hanging with geeks," Kara says.

"Did I mention she has a nose ring?" We both laugh. "I'll call her right now."

Even though I'm exhausted from our all-nighter, I get up early before school and check on our now-completed science project. After homework last night we begged Dad to take a quick trip to Home Depot. Dad helped us by staying up late and building something called a cold frame for the plants in his newly buffed-out workshop in the garage. The cold frame is basically a wooden box with no bottom, and it has a piece of clear acrylic glass on a hinged top to protect the plants. He built two identical ones. They are side by side, one with the words WAR, HATE, DESTRUCTION painted in black letters on the front and the other says PEACE, LOVE, GRATITUDE on it, painted in purple and with little colored peace sign and butterfly stickers all around the letters. Using some of Dad's old set lights we lit up the back yard like daytime and we worked till one in the morning, first measuring the dirt and the water so each squash plant has the exact same growing medium and we put three seeds in each plastic pot. We set up a big lidded bucket for the water and we will measure it out to give the exact same amount for each plant every time we water. We have six pots in each cold frame. I'm excited about the project. When I dip the measuring cup in the bucket to water I focus on the words painted on the side of the cold frame and send that message to each plant. I want to talk to the plants like I do the others in the garden but I refrain, knowing it could contaminate our scientific results. I open both of the cold frames one inch to allow ventilation. After school Kara will come and close the cold frames and water again, and she'll also send the words written on the cold frames mentally to the plants. Every three days we have to photograph the plants to record our results.

I clean up and get dressed, ready for my second day back at school. I'm not even worried about what people will say about me today. Let them talk. What do I care?

Chapter Twenty-six

Time marches on, they say. Whatever that means. The plants continue to grow in the cold frames in my backyard. In the three weeks since we started our science fair experiment I have come to hate, really loathe, the plants in the War and Destruction cold frame. They are eeky, oily little buggers, twisted and deformed, but they are still growing like the cockroaches that they are. I'm appalled at myself for not being able to love them or to give them any comfort when I send them thoughts about war, hate, and destruction. Kara tells me she feels the same way about them.

In the Hippie cold frame, as we call it, the love and peace thoughts have brought us forth a bouquet of darling squash plants that curl and vine around their little box home with abandon. Kara and I are in love with these plants and we are both shocked that our experiment has worked, and we are really proud of ourselves for the amount of time and commitment that we've put into it. Mrs. Bandy, the science teacher, came and looked at our experiment because Suzi told her about it. She is really impressed with us, which feels great.

I write in my journal about this and other things. It's been the best month I've had in a long time. Jimmy has been a dull ache that plagues me sometimes, especially when I see him at school and he bats his eyes at me in a sad way. I've even cried a few times over him. And sometimes I wake up with a start thinking that I'm missing an appointment with Michael, and then I remember I don't see him anymore. It's really weird that these spirits still haunt me, ghost pains like missing appendages that I can still feel.

Outside the day sparkles bright as LA days do, and I pine for The Granddaughter. She hasn't come to see me in a long time and I fear she is unable to return to me. I wrack my brains trying to remember what she said to me last-- her words have been swallowed up by each passing day. I call out to her mentally and she doesn't come. It's like empty nest syndrome, that thing my mom's friend has because her college-age daughter moved out and after years of being a soccer mom, she's now all alone.

Science fair day turns out to be a bigger deal to me than I thought it would be. Kara and I carefully pack up our plants and the cold frames in Mom's minivan. We bring the colorful cardboard display that includes photographs documenting the growth of our plants and the way we conducted the experiment. Some of the War plants have died, and all but one of our Hippie plants are thriving

155

beyond expectation. Suzi says there's a lot of buzz in the science club about our project, so when we get to school a whole bunch of science geeks come and help us unload everything and carry it to the gym. We quickly set up our display in an area marked "Biology" and then go and wander around and look at the other entries. There are more than I thought there would be . . . at least 200.

"All the sophomores in biology had to participate," says Suzi as Kara and I walk around with her. "And a lot of people want the twenty extra credit points for their science grades. Like you."

I smile. That was originally my intent, but since then science has sort of sparked my interest and now my grade is going to be a B anyway.

"There's Jimmy," I say in a low voice to Kara and Suzi.

Kara sighs. "He's a real hottie." I smack her arm. "Well he is!"

I look him up and down and he glances over at me then looks back to Cristabelle, who, in a putrid twist of fate, he's hooked up with.

"Yeah, he is fine, damn him!" I agree. We all giggle as we meander down the makeshift aisles grouped loosely as Biology and Earth Sciences, Chemistry and Physics, and Engineering.

There are some interesting experiments, I have to admit. I'm surprised by what kids at my school have come up with. There are projects on global warming, water pollution, black holes, and some bizarre stuff like something called a parallax, the effects of cooking with fresh vs. canned pineapples, the heat coagulation of egg proteins, and even a description of why the sky is blue.

The school bell rings but it's Saturday so we know it means that judging will start soon and we need to get back to our display in case the judges have questions. I clutch Kara's arm as we head toward the Biology aisle.

"See ya," Suzi says as she ducks into the Physics aisle. "Good luck!" I beam at her. The gym comes alive with nervous excitement. I see my mom and dad in the bleachers and wave at them from our booth.

Next to us a cute guy with long black dreadlocks is still setting up his display boards. I can't tell what nationality he is other than he has beautiful latte-colored arms. I find myself staring at him almost trance-like until Kara nudges me. He looks up and smiles. His teeth are white and even, really beautiful. It makes me wish I'd been to the dentist more.

"Hi," he says to me, and I actually feel light-headed, he's so good looking. Kara nudges me again. I realize I haven't answered him and I blush.

"Oh . . . hi," I say. We both laugh.

"Uh . . . cool project. I got so busy reading yours that I forgot to set mine up." He smiles again and I get that deja vu, the-universe-is-one kind of feeling.

"Thanks," I say. "I'm Jessie. This is Kara."

"Taz," he says, smiling again. We shake hands for some reason.

I think I'm in love.

The judges finally round the corner and Kara and I anxiously hop from foot to foot while we wait for them to come to our table. They look at our project and read all about Dr. Emoto's experiment with water that inspired us. The judges, all professors from UCLA, look at one another and nod. Mrs. Bandy, who is escorting them, winks at me and Kara. The judges check a few marks off on their clipboard sheets and walk away without asking us any questions. Now we just have to wait.

Chapter Twenty-seven

On Monday morning I meet Kara next to the Alumni Museum at school. Since she is the only one from Amelia Earhart Continuation High School who entered the science fair, she was given a day pass to attend Hollywood High for the science fair results. I like seeing her on our campus as she walks toward me, all goth and cool with her tatts and black makeup. She nervously squeezes my hand when we meet.

"I haven't stepped foot on this campus for two years since I got kicked out, except for the gym this weekend."

"Well, you're back!" I say with a "here's Johnny" grin. "Let's go to the assembly, or we'll never get a seat."

We wedge our backpacks into the crowd to carve a path towards the auditorium.

"Hey, guess what? My dad came back. He drove me here. He's parking the car but he's going to watch the results."

Kara looks happy and I smile.

"Cool!" I tell her as we enter the auditorium. "My mom and dad are here somewhere too."

It seems so normal; our parents here to support us as we wait for our science fair results. Less than a year ago I could never have made up this scenario, Kara and me together at an academic event we both participated in. We push our way inside as the entire student body finds seats on the hard metal chairs, glad to be ditching their first period class. I wonder how my parents will even get through the door, it's so dog-eat-dog. As we finally find a place to park ourselves, a familiar voice distracts me.

"This seat taken?" I look up and it is Taz. I shake my head.

"Go ahead," I say. Kara elbows me hard in the arm and I elbow her back. Taz smiles as he sits down.

"So, where did you come from? Before you moved here, I mean," I can't help asking him. I've never seen him at school before this weekend. Was I so in love with Jimmy that I just didn't look at other guys?

"I'm a transfer," he says. "I just came here in September, from a small town in Northern California. Dorris, up near the Oregon border. You probably haven't heard of it. If you're ever up that way, you should stop by. Dorris is well known as the town with the tallest flagpole west of the Mississippi."

"Oh," I say, smiling at the town's claim to fame. "Cool." He's so close I can smell his scent. Taz smells almost as good as Jimmy.

Mrs. Bandy, the "Fair Chair" as we call her, goes up to the podium and taps on the microphone. We wait through long announcements and congratulations, and all that boring stuff adults like to say when they have an audience.

159

A few special mention prizes are awarded so now there are kids sitting up on the stage with Mrs. Bandy, looking uncomfortable as they hold their trophies in their laps and wait.

There are three awards for each science fair category so it seems like it takes forever for the Biology results to be announced. At least Suzi and a couple of her sci-squad won first place for their physics project so we have someone to cheer for. Otherwise, I don't know any of the kids called up to accept their prizes. It's like this entire segment of the school population has somehow missed my radar. I guess I was too busy macking on Jimmy and fighting Evil Cheerleaders from Hell to notice them.

In the midst of millions of bodies squirming around in their seats, my heart feels like it's pounding up to my throat when Mrs. Bandy makes the announcement. "And finally, in biology, we had some very creative projects this year. All of you deserve congratulations. But unfortunately there are only three prizes in biology. The third place winner for an interesting project on the 11th dimension using the membrane theory is: Catherine Wong."

Catherine, a senior, goes up to get her prize. Kara and I hold hands tightly, our hearts thumping wildly. Could we have gotten second place?

"And in second place for a convincing argument against owls using echolocation, the prize goes to Wanda Keller, Shannon O'Shea, and Brett Nissan," Mrs. Bandy continues. Kara and I look at each other, feeling a bit sick. Were we wrong about the looks that we saw the judges give us? Were we mistaken about the other students' excitement over our project? Or could we have really won first place? We hold our breath. My armpits are sweating, I'm so nervous. Shannon, Wanda and Brett take forever to worm their way

160

up to the stage and get their trophy and photo taken. "And the first place award in biology " . . . I swear I can't breathe-- "for a fascinating demonstration of global warming, goes to Tazura Badjeerian!" I feel like I'm underwater all of sudden, and my heart sinks and my cheeks flush hot and red. I'm more than a little embarrassed that my parents talked me into letting them come here today, only to watch me lose. It reminds me of the audition list for the holiday show at the dance studio, when we all ran up to the posting to see what parts we got. Instead of getting Clara in The Nutcracker-- the part I desperately wanted--next to my name it said "Soldier #1", which was worse than nothing. This feels exactly the same way but I keep my face expressionless as Kara stares moodily into her lap. We have no clue who Tazura Badjeerian is so we look around the gym, trying to act like it doesn't matter that we lost. But all of sudden Taz is standing up next to us and trying to get to the aisle.

"Oh, hey!" I say, finally figuring out that Taz is short for Tazura. I'm happy it's him, but I'm also really disappointed. We clap for Taz as he retrieves his trophy and certificate (wishing it was us). I try not to seem like I'm upset as Taz walks up to the stage, holds up his trophy in this cute shy way, and sits down on the metal chair awaiting him near Mrs. Bandy. I just want to get out of there now, and I hope I don't see my parents. I feel really bad for Kara, who got the special pass to be there and invited her dad on top of it. Crap.

Mrs. Bandy returns to the microphone and mindlessly taps it again before talking. Kara and I roll our eyes in disgust. Will this torture ever end? After a seriously long inhale, Mrs. Bandy says, "And lastly, we would like to announce our special award, the Scientific Innovation Award." Kara is putting her satchel over her shoulders, ready to walk out and go back to her own school. I don't blame her. I would leave too if my parents weren't there somewhere, waiting to see me.

"This trophy is for overall achievement and innovation, and is given to a student participating in any category. In this case it is for two students, for their project on plant growth using positive versus negative reinforcement. Please come forward, Kara Slauson and Jessica Allen. Congratulations, girls!"

I feel my brain spinning as I try to grasp what just happened. *Me?* Kara looks even more shocked than I am, I think she wasn't really paying attention and doesn't know what award we just won. She smiles at me nervously and points at herself, her blackened eyes raised in a question mark, and I nod and we help each other up. I can feel all eyes on us as we walk down the longest aisle ever and up the stage stairs into the blinding theater lights. There is a roar of sound coming from the seats and I am surprised. Do these people know us? I realize it is Suzi's group, the science- geek squad, clapping loudly for us as we nervously approach the microphone. My throat has closed shut so I'm glad we don't have to speak. Kara is clutching onto my shirt as Mrs. Bandy hands us our trophy, a really big one, bigger than the others. Our names are engraved on the front. I can barely hear Mrs. Bandy thanking everyone for coming and supporting the Hollywood High Science Club as I stare at the trophy.

"Great job!" Mrs. Bandy says to us, giving me a sideways hug and shaking Kara's hand. Everything's a blur as we stand there holding the trophy, posing for photos for the school newspaper and yearbook, first just the two of us and then the entire group of winners smile for the camera as the audience clears the room. After the photo shoot Taz comes

162

over and gives me a hug. He gives Kara one too but mine is longer.

"Nice going," he says.

"You too."

I'm still buzzing from the high of it all when I overhear two freshmen girls as they collect their backpacks and shoulder their trophies, ready to leave the stage.

"That's the girl who tried to kill herself," one says. I can see the other one look me over from the corner of my eye.

"Nah," she says. "That's not her. That's the science girl. That suicide girl doesn't go here anymore, remember? She got kicked out."

"Oh, yeah," the first girl says. "Didn't she get kicked out for having sex in the locker room with some football player?"

"Ew!" the other one says.

Wow, I think. *What a trip*. Now I'm the Science Girl. Who knew?

My parents descend on us with camera and smiles. Keith even stays and waves at me and gives me a thumbs up before jetting off to class. We pose for a few more photos, and I've never seen my dad look more proud. Mom is even smiling broadly, something she hasn't done in years. We shake Principal Asshole's hand and after he excuses himself Mom hugs me and Dad picks me up and spins me around, he's so excited.

"We'll see you at home, sweetie. Who's taking the trophy first?" He winks at Kara.

"Jess can have it first," Kara says, "But we'll for sure trade off!"

"Can you take it?" I ask Dad. I don't want to carry it around all day; even though I'm proud to have won it that would be too embarrassing. Dad nods and tucks it under his arm like a surfboard. Mom rolls her eyes at him as they wave goodbye to us. Kara's dad stands shyly at the foot of the stairs leading to the stage, and I see Mom shaking hands with him. He checks out the trophy and chats with my parents before they walk out together.

"We did it!" Kara says. "I can't believe we won!"

"I didn't think we were going to win anything, I was so mad I was going to leave!"

"I know! I saw you getting ready to go and then they called our names!" Kara and I are rehashing the whole thing in minute detail, stunned by our luck, when Taz walks up. I didn't know he was waiting for us.

"Oh, hi!" I say, smiling. I squeeze his arm; I'm so excited I'm actually giddy.

"Hey! I'm really happy for you guys," he says.

"You too! You did great!" Now that we won too I really am happy for him. I can't stop smiling.

"Ready to go to second period?" Taz asks. "I mean, I could walk you to class."

Kara's eyes get big and she beams at me.

"Uh, sure!" I say, and I smile even more. Kara's dad stops at the door and motions for her to come with him. The spell is broken, and now she needs to go back to her own school. We walk back to our seats and she gets her satchel. I hug her for the tenth time.

"Thanks," she whispers into my ear. I nod, feeling strangely emotional. This doesn't feel like my life, but I like it.

"See you later?"

"Sure."

Kara's dad puts his arm around her shoulders and Taz and I wave. We are alone in the auditorium except for the janitor, who is quickly folding up chairs.

"We'd better go or we'll be late," Taz says. I nod and we leave together, feeling like old friends.

Chapter Twenty-eight

I'm sitting at the desk in my bedroom cramming for an English test on a beautiful Saturday afternoon when I hear an odd noise. It sounds a lot like a static-y radio or something. I look around and I'm shocked to see The Granddaughter. She is an outline of herself, barely there. It takes awhile before I can see her better and her thoughts fill mine, like a slow Internet connection.

"Hello Jessica," she says.

"Oh my gosh! How are you? I haven't seen you in so long!" I want to hug her; I'm so overcome with emotion to see her. Her chevron smile brings tears to my eyes.

"I have missed you as well, Jessica. It has been difficult to return to you."

"Are you having problems on your spaceship?" I ask, realizing right away what a completely ridiculous question that is. Again the chevron smile.

"Let me show you . . . " and she reaches her bluish-grey hand over to my temple and my mind is instantly filled with a 3-D tour of her world. The tour is a model, not the real place but a replica of where she lives. The "spaceship" is more like a city, a beautiful, enclosed city with trees and flowers and birds and walkways and meandering paths. There are no people but I can feel what their presence would be like, and it is very different from the human energy of my time, it is focused and intelligent and spiritual. An artificial sun hangs above me as I move through the mental 3-D replica and I somehow know the entirety of how this place has come to be. . . this false earth is the size of a small star, a planet of its own contained and made of ingredients from the mother planet, Earth.

It is the new home of humanity, at least until Earth has recovered from the pollution and destruction and chaos from many millennia of human inhabitants. Here there are living spaces and classrooms and places for nourishment and entertainment but the place is peacefully quiet except for the interchange of thoughts, an interchange that I somehow understand anyone can go in and out of at will. There are no secrets here. Communication is largely achieved by brain waves. The entire place has a life force of its own. I can tell that the "spaceship" is somehow a living being, sustainable and aware. I have never experienced anything like it . . . it is an all-new thing to me. The feeling I get more than anything else is the sensation of deep concern that the inhabitants of this place have for Earth. They are the guardians of the future of the planet, and they are all a part of me somehow. We are connected. I finally understand now what The Granddaughter meant when she said there is no such thing as time. She is right, we are a continuation of each other but not separate from each other. We are all One.

Suddenly we are back in my bedroom at my desk and The Granddaughter is smiling in a pleased but sad way.

"You are saying goodbye to me now, aren't you?" I ask, wondering if I picked up the ability to psychically communicate by being with her.

"I am," she says. "I must leave. It has been a great struggle to get you to this point in your life space, Jessica. But it has been accomplished. My goal is achieved."

"What goal?"

"You living your life. There are many, many realities, many paths a life may take. Your living was one path but since most of your paths ended in your death at a young age, it has taken much concentrated effort to find you in the life space in which you actually lived past the age of sixteen. And in our previous attempts to find you we found only your family mourning your death."

Hearing these words now shocks me somehow. I hated to be mean to the War and Destruction plants in my experiment but yet here less than a year before I was willing to take my own life, to kill myself. I vow silently to never hurt myself again, not even with mean thoughts, now that I know firsthand that mean thoughts can be as bad as mean actions. The Granddaughter touches my arm, and the contrast of our colors make me wonder what race she is.

We are one race, she reminds me mentally. Humanity will become a streamlined entity of Oneness, One people. All people are all bloods.

Somehow that thought gives me comfort but the sadness of losing her starts to overcome me. I don't want her to leave me.

168

"There's so much I still want to learn. . ."

"You have fulfilled your destiny," The Granddaughter assures me. "You will live."

"I will miss you."

"Goodbye, Grandmother," she tells me.

She has never called me that before.

My Granddaughter touches my temple and looks at me with a knowingness that spans the ages before she disappears with a jaggedy blue-gray shimmer.

I'm sitting at my desk cramming for my English test on a beautiful Saturday afternoon, but the words of the tragic tale I'm reading float up around me, couched in incomprehensible 'thees' and 'thous'. The bedroom door opens. Kara and Suzi walk in. I'm a little disoriented and for some reason I feel very sad. That must be what the author was going for when he wrote this tragedy. I smile up at my friends, glad for a break. Why are they here? Did we have a study date?

"What's up?" I ask, trying to remember if we had plans.

"We're going shopping on Sunset and you're coming. Taz has some super hot cousins in town and he's taking them to show them the boulevard."

"How do you know?" I ask.

"He called . . . duh!" Suzi says, pointing to her cell phone. "He called you first but your phone is going haywire, it didn't even ring."

I stand up from my chair, and I feel light headed. I start to remember the strangest dream I had last night that doesn't seem like a dream about a tall willowy figure, someone I know well. I wish I could remember. It's all a strange blur. I pick up my phone and look at it . . . one missed call. When did I miss a call? I was right here studying. Maybe I did fall asleep at my desk and I'm just waking up.

"You okay? You look a little . . . sick," Suzi comments.

"Yeah," Kara agrees. "You look different. Maybe not sick, but--you're glowing!"

"Jessie's in love," Suzi singsongs, and Kara pokes her and they laugh.

I'm still woozy as I struggle to remember. What's going on? I have the most uncanny feeling that something profound happened to me just now, but for the life of me I can't say what it is.

"I don't know . . . I feel like I'm forgetting something," I say.

"You are!" Suzi says. "You're forgetting the hot boys we're going to casually and accidentally not bump into while we shop on Sunset!"

I smile but I can't shake that nagging feeling --what is it?

"I'm coming with you! But I wish I could remember. It was something . . . a dream I had last night about a lady I was talking to . . . she was blue."

"Sad?" Suzi asks.

"Color," I say.

"Oh."

Kara grabs my arm and pulls me away from the desk chair.

"There has obviously been too much of this studying," she says as she closes my English lit book. "It's starting to affect your brain."

"The Blue Lady?" Suzi chimes in. "Now you are being haunted by Technicolor ghosts? C'mon, Jess! Get with the program! We said there are *boys* to find on The Strip! And

170

your über-cute boyfriend Taz is one of them! Grab your lip gloss and let's go!"

I pop a breath mint in my mouth and shake away the lingering thoughts of the strange blue lady I keep thinking I should know and run a comb through my hair. There's no sense in protesting, the boys *are* waiting. I barely have a chance to grab my purse before my two best friends pull me out the bedroom door.

The Time Traveler's Chronicle
By Cat Spydell

Sequel to
The Time Traveler's Apprentice

Coming
November 2012

About the Author

Cat Spydell is a writer, editor, and publisher who lives in Palos Verdes, CA, where she raises her two teenaged children. When she is not working on her writing and publishing projects, she can be found at the horse barn, in the ocean on her bodyboard, or puttering around in her garden. She is the co-author of *A Circle of Horses* and author of the upcoming young adult novel *Epona's Gift*.